Seductive Characters

Episodes 1-4: Breaking The 4th Wall Season One

Melody Grace Hicks

Description

How much trouble can one erotic romance writer get into? Maybe I shouldn't have agreed to the Faustian deal with Loki, but you try turning him down!

***

All writers say their fictional characters talk to them. Mine jumped through the fabric of reality. But it's not like there's a writing course on preparing for your character's sudden appearance in your backyard. Now that Asgard's Dark Prince has opened the door between universes, he isn't my only fictional character to do so. It's all well and good to design traits of dominant sexy gods that are mouth-wateringly built with lickable muscles, fantasy warrior proportions in every respect—yeah, you know what I'm talking about—and those panty-melting voices...

until they turn their sights on me. What's a writer to do but hold on for the ride and document the chaos as they turn my once quiet life upside down?

After all, inspiration comes in many forms.

This compilation includes the first four episodes of Breaking The 4th Wall Season One: A Writer's Commitment (Episode 1); Delayed Gratification (Episode 2); Don't Taunt The Trickster (Episode 3); and Ladies' Night (Episode 4).

Contents

Ladies' Night

This is a work of fiction. The names, characters, places, and incidents are products of my imagination or have been used fictitiously and are not to be construed as real. Yikes, what does that say about me? Any resemblance to persons, living or dead, is entirely coincidental. Characters included in this story are from my own novels (*Gallows Tree Conspiracy, Hidden—Triquetra Trilogy Book One*); however, I have allowed them to visit and merge across my different story universes within the environment of my fourth wall-breaking interactions. These tales are told from the perspective of the writer and wrangler of these characters. I will absolutely poke fun at an entirely fictional version of myself as my characters cause trouble.

Within these episodes, I've included characters that encompass numerous world mythologies. However, these are deliberately manipulated into the needs of the fictional universes I've developed. They absolutely do not represent the real-world beliefs of any one group, nor are they intended to accurately reflect, impinge, or denigrate any of these real-world mythologies or cultures.

Trigger Warnings: Overconsumption of alcohol, cheating, stalking, and references to death of a loved one.

Content themes/tropes: Polyamory, bondage, dominance, submission, masochism, exhibitionism, size differences, explicit sexual language, edging, denial, food play, water play, possessive, alpha hero, emotional scars, different worlds, and three's a crowd.

I take no responsibility or liability for any damage, injury, or loss of any personal property including but not limited to unemployment, furniture breakage, walking into a telephone pole while reading, toy purchases, or spontaneous combustion of panties stemming from reading these tales. Read at your own risk. For those who decide to dive in, I highly recommend proximity to towels, a change of panties, cold showers, and fire extinguishers at all times. This is an erotic romance! It is spicy! You might want to make sure no one is reading over your shoulder on the bus, train, university/college classroom, or office. And good god, don't try to read this while driving!

Checked over your shoulder? All clear? With those warnings out of the way, let's dive in, shall we?

A Writer's Commitment

Episode One Description

How much trouble can one erotic romance writer get into? Maybe I shouldn't have agreed to the Faustian deal with Loki, but you try turning him down!

***

All writers say their fictional characters talk to them. Mine jumped through the fabric of reality. But it's not like there's a writing course on preparing for your fictional character's sudden appearance in your backyard. Now that Asgard's Dark Prince has opened the door between universes, he isn't my only fictional character to do so. What's a writer to do but document the chaos as they turn my once quiet life upside down.

After all, inspiration comes in many forms.

CHAPTER ONE

Authenticity Is Key

I f life takes a left turn into the unexplainable, would you allow yourself to enjoy the journey or insist on trying to make sense of it?

The morning sun warms my skin as I swing gently, sitting sideways in my hammock on the sand by the dock. Like the water lapping at the nearby shore, the words pour in effortless waves of inspiration. With a grin, I click the enter button and send the first chapter to my beta-readers. It's my newest story idea, *Hidden*, part of an exciting universe of stories revolving around the idea that gods and beings from mythology are real and living hidden among us.

A shadow on my face disrupts my concentration as the loss of warmth sends a shiver down my back in the cool fall air. My gaze flicks up from my computer screen, and

I squeak, jerking my body back and setting the hammock swaying.

The dark silhouette of a male is only a couple of metres from me, the sun creating a halo around him.

My heart races, and it takes me a minute to close my gaping mouth. Thoughts spinning, I narrow my gaze to focus on the here and now, yet half my mind is still partly immersed in my fictional universe and its wealth of individuals.

I lick my lips with a mouth gone dry and attempt a weak chuckle. "Are you real, or are you one of my characters?" I ask the tall figure before me.

I'm only partly kidding. He's standing in front of me, so, of course, he's real, right? *Right*? Because if he isn't actually there, how is he casting a shadow on me? Although, maybe I've fallen asleep, and this is a dream? In dreams, it's perfectly fine to speak with my fictional characters.

After all, one hazard of being a writer is getting lost in one's imagination and I've definitely had fun creating my latest male protagonist from a blend of gods from numerous new-world and old-world pantheons. Who wouldn't want to write about a shapeshifting trickster powered by sex, stories, and chaos?

But no, I still smell the freshly cut grass, feel the light breeze stirring my hair, and the warmth of the sun contrasting with the cooler air. I bite my lip. This has to be real. It's too vivid to be a dream.

And now he must think I'm nuts. I roll my eyes at myself, barely holding back my snort. It's probably the Amazon delivery guy needing a signature. Although, speaking of crazy things, how did he get through my backyard and all the way to the water without my noticing? I'm not that oblivious when writing, am I?

Looking at the evidence in front of me, maybe I am.

His head cocks to the side as he considers his answer.

Squinting, my eyes start to adjust to the difference between the bright sky behind him and his face and body in shadow, but I still can't quite make out any details of his features. Judging by his silhouette, he is tall and athletically built, but leanly muscled, not bulky. The sun reflects off parts of his clothes with a metallic glare, while other areas have a sheen suggesting leather.

With every new visual clue, my heartbeat quickens. *Armour? Leather? A quarterback's build? That's not... no, it's not possible.* Thoughts swirling, my gaze flicks from my computer screen's description of Asgard's Dark Prince to the male in front of me several times in succession. *It can't be. Really?*

"I believe—"

My breath breaks in a small gasp as he begins to speak in a sexy posh accent, the same lilt I've chosen for my Asgardians. *No way!*

"—that I would consider myself real in some planes of existence and one of your characters in other multiversal realities... since you decided to write a novel including the God of Stories," he says in his purring baritone.

He walks closer in a predator's prowl, full of confidence and swagger, stopping only when his legs bump my crossed shins in the hammock.

I know my mouth is hanging open, but I can't help it. Finally able to see him fully, he is heart-stoppingly gorgeous—my imagination brought to life. Thick, shoulder-length black hair frames his pale angular face. Thin red lips turn up in a half-smile and penetrating green eyes, cat-bright and by no means tame, are set off by long, dark lashes. I can barely wrap my mind around the sight of him here, in front of me.

His hand reaches for me and long narrow fingers catch my chin, tilting my head up to meet those intense eyes. "You called to me, little writer," he adds as he takes in my features. Everywhere his gaze travels, it leaves shivery prickles of sensation in its wake.

Gooseflesh breaks out over my skin, and I rub my hands over my upper arms.

"Should I..." I swallow and lick my lips in an attempt to speak past a suddenly dry mouth. "Should I apologize for that?" My voice cracks a bit at the end.

His smile slowly broadens, and his eyes turn mischievous, half-lidded and crinkling at the corners. "That depends. Are you willing to pay the consequences of attracting my attention?" His thumb caresses my cheek where he still holds my chin, sending shivers along my spine.

I gnaw my lower lip before answering. "What... what are the consequences?"

Releasing me, he licks his own lip, biting it as he presses my laptop closed and moves it to the ground. With fingers wrapping around each of my ankles, he uncrosses my legs and steps between them. He leans over, with his hands gripping the fabric on either side of the hammock by my head. He pushes into my space until his breath tickles my face with every exhale.

"I demand authenticity. I am a God, after all, and not just of Stories, as you are well aware. Your imagination alone is insufficient to provide the inspiration and accuracy you require to adequately represent me within your stories. I have high standards. If you are going to describe how I look, my appearance, my expressions and reactions, then I insist you give me your time and attention to do your research properly."

I can't help but tremble with him so close, so overwhelming to my senses, and oh god, so very male. He's everything I find attractive. His scent is a combination of freshly cut conifer forests, hand-tanned leather, and citrus fruit, sweet like oranges. His aura radiates strength, dominance with an edge of danger, and heat. Even with my moratorium on relationships after finding my ex balls-deep within another, it makes my libido sit up and take notice. Deadly to panties everywhere, he exudes sex appeal in spades.

I nod my agreement, not sure I can utter a sound. Or worse, that my words will come out in a squeak.

"Oh no, little writer. I need to hear your voice. Your verbal agreement that you will give me your time and attention," he demands, his tone a low growl and his eyes not leaving mine.

Barely able to suck in more than shallow gasps, my body is flushed and achy with desire.

"Yes," I manage in a breathless whisper. I try again. "Yes," I get out, a bit louder.

The flash of a satisfied smile, so quick I almost miss the expression and then he is in motion.

One hand fists my hair at the nape of my neck, partly bracing my back, as the other arm scoops under my ass, lifting me effortlessly out of the hammock to press my core tight against his body. My legs wrap around his hips instinctively.

He's undeniably aroused, large and rigid against the thin protection of my yoga pants. I can barely focus. His mouth hovers just out of touching distance of mine. If I move my face a fraction, I could press our lips together. Despite the pull on my hair, I strain towards him, wanting, no... needing to close that distance. God, it's been a few years since I kissed someone. I haven't wanted to. Not like this... this yearning that's a fire inside me.

He tugs my head back a bit further, a small smirk betraying his amusement as his eyes glitter with restrained lust.

"You understand that means if you are writing a scene where I ravage a character's tiny pussy with this thick cock"—he grinds aggressively against me, and I moan at the flare of heat within me—"fucking her hard and deep, pounding her until she can't walk, or making her cum so many times she passes out, I expect you to experience it first. You have to know how it feels to gag on it when I shove it down your throat, to know what I taste like when I fill you full of cum, what it feels like to drip down your thighs. I'll make sure you enjoy it, of course, but I will tie you up, tease your body, control your pleasure, and teach you the value of walking the tightrope of a little pain to enhance the pleasure. Are you sure you understand and agree to all that?"

I swallow, blinking up at him. No one has ever spoken to me like this before, and fuck, it's hot. It's got me so aroused I'm positive he must be able to feel how wet I am, soaking through my panties, my pants, and into his leather as he continues to grind his cock against me. My pulse throbs, a second heartbeat in my sex. Between his actions and filthy language, he's going to have me orgasming fully clothed.

"Oh god... Yes, I understand," I whimper.

His eyes darken further. "Oh, and I will fuck this tight little ass as well. Say 'Yes, Loki' so I know you agree, little writer."

Heat expands as my inner thighs tremble. I swallow hard. "Yes, Loki."

His mouth lowers, nipping my lower lip. "You are mine, little writer. Time for your first lesson."

CHAPTER TWO

First Lesson

His tongue eases the sting from his teeth with a caress of my lip. Despite his unyielding grip on my hair, he's not hurting me. Our lips touch and I'm lost in the sensation of warmth, the teasing glide along the seam of my mouth, the stroke of tongue against tongue. Not a battle or plundering. Instead, it's a coaxing draw to pull me deeper, a dance, a partnership that effortlessly twirls me into the depths of seductive pleasure.

My head spins, dizzy with both the feelings he's so easily evoking and a lack of air. But I don't want to break the kiss, even as the demand in my lungs grows, competing with the honeyed thrum in my veins.

His lips lift from mine and my eyes flutter open, blinking, as a mewl of protest escapes me.

"Where is your bedroom? I could have taken you on the grass, and I will in the future, but this time, our first time, I want you completely comfortable," he purrs.

I hadn't realized we were moving until now, but looking beyond him, we've entered my home, and he's climbing the staircase to the second floor.

"First door on the right," I answer, and having reached the top of the stairs, he pushes the door open.

His smooth strides take us to my king-sized bed and he leans over to press me down onto the blankets. Those clever lips lower again and my pulse leaps to reignite our kiss. He's so much larger than I, even though I don't consider myself small. Yet he surrounds me, grinding against my sex in a way that has me arching up to close the slight distance between our chests.

Cool metal meets my bare skin, but in the next moment, it's warm flesh as he rids himself of his armour, doublet, and tunic. I hadn't noticed when he'd unbuttoned my shirt or removed my bra, but as his fingertips close over one breast, plucking at my nipple, a gasp leaves my mouth for his. His lips curve and he nips his way to my ear, licking and scraping his teeth and sending shudders to meld the sparking sensations from his mouth, his fingers, and his cock into a fiery heat in my abdomen.

"Please, Loki," I beg, one of my hands leaving his hair to explore the firm muscles flexing in his shoulder, his arm, then his chest and abdomen. His fingers catch mine before I can do more than brush his pants.

"All in good time, little writer," he says, his mouth moving down my neck, over my collarbone and before I lose my breath as his lips close over my nipple.

"Oh god," I whimper, feeling the draw of his mouth like a string connected between my nipple and clit. With every pull, he's tightening, coiling my arousal higher.

I'm trembling, a fine sweat breaks out on my skin. So close... damn it, I'm so close.

He releases my nipple, moving down my body. "Not yet. Not until I've tasted you, darling."

Before I can finish my protesting whine, he's stripped my pants and panties from me. Seeing his broad shoulders between my thighs, those emerald eyes dark with lust, my sex clenches, my pulse pounding in my ears, and I grip the bedding around me. Anticipation shimmers in my belly.

He draws a deep breath through his nose, a visible shudder shaking him, then pins me with his half-lidded gaze.

"Your scent—fuck, you smell delicious. I'm trying to restrain myself, not fucking pound you into the mattress this first time, but Norns, little writer... you have me harder than Yggdrasil's heartwood."

His tone lowers into a growl that has me biting my lip with a whimper, fisting the blankets, and tilting my hips. God, I want him to pound me into my mattress.

"Please, Loki." My voice is a choked whisper, but it still draws his smile.

"I do love hearing you beg," he purrs.

Then his mouth lowers to lick the length of my folds and I cry out at the lightning spearing me, shaking in reaction. With a snarl, his tongue lathes my clit.

A shriek rips from my throat, my body bucking as the climax explodes across my senses.

Yet he doesn't stop. Instead, he laps at my release. Then, just as I think I might catch a full breath from my seizing lungs, he returns to my clit, sucking it between his lips.

"Oh, *fuck!*" I scream as the new orgasm sears up my spine to turn my vision white.

My sex is still spasming when he shifts up and surges inside with one savage drive of his hips. Almost painful with the full stretching, but it just prolongs the cascading pleasure. My eyes roll back in my head as guttural moans fall from my lips. Loki's hissed inhale and groan are muffled through the thundering in my ears.

When the shudders ease, I open my eyes to look into Loki's darkened gaze, his body braced above me.

"Are you back with me?" He slowly draws his hips up until only the tip of his cock is still within me. "I want you to feel every single stroke of my cock in this tight little cunt of yours."

Just as slowly, he drives his cock deep again and I moan.

"I want you to be fully aware of who is inside you, who is fucking this luscious little body, stretching it to fit," he growls, still holding my gaze.

"You, Loki. It's you," I whimper.

He smiles, thrusting faster.

"Yes. Me. Who does this sexy little body belong to?"

"You, Loki."

My breath pants as his hips snap with each thrust, hitting my clit and driving his cock to the hilt every time. Heat spreads from my core, another orgasm gathering steam, and god, his possessive words and tone make it all the hotter. Whether it is his shape or experience, his cock rubs along my G-spot and hits that sensitive patch near my cervix in a dual onslaught. It has my walls quivering, closer to the edge with every stroke.

"Are you going to cum for me again, little writer? Squeeze my cock even tighter?"

I attempt to answer, but my words stutter. The air is arrested as my lungs seize, my spine bowing as the climax detonates.

Loki snarls, thrusting harder with the slap of skin on skin. My legs are already wrapped around his hips, but he takes one, shoving my knee up towards my chest as he fucks me faster.

I can't catch my breath, gasping, my body shaking as another wave overtakes me, then another, swamping me in sensation. Never before have I orgasmed repeatedly and the ocean of pleasure has me clinging to Loki, my only solid source of reference, my guide in these uncharted waters. My cries of completion barely register to my ears.

Until Loki's roar blasts through the fog.

The heated gush floods my core, every twitch of his cock sending ripples through me, and I pant as it sets off another series of climactic waves.

Rocking in the aftermath, it takes a while for my brain to kick in, but when it does, my first thought blurts out of my mouth between breaths. "Wow... that was... I've never... that was amazing."

Loki lifts his head, a smile appearing as he takes in my expression. I must look a mess—red-faced, sweating, panting. He's not out of breath, damn it, although his chest is still heaving slightly. Fingers caress my cheek as his eyelids lower to partially shield his gaze, pupils expanding and eating the gemstone green. His lips quirk into a lopsided smirk.

"Oh darling, you didn't think I was done yet, did you? I'm a god"—he thrusts his hips and I suck in a sharp breath as I feel his cock completely hard within me—"and I have so much more to teach you."

CHAPTER THREE

Unexpected

Two weeks have passed since Loki began visiting me, changing my perspective on reality. He's been here every day, popping into my world at will, since he first showed up that memorable Friday. Each time, he leaves tangible evidence behind in the satiated exhaustion of my body, his scent surrounding me, and fluids between my thighs. I'm certainly not dreaming his presence.

And wow, it's been inspiring.

The story flows fast from my fingertips as I incorporate everything he's taught me about himself, building on the traits I'd already given him. Despite his explanation of multiple universes and multiple versions of himself, I still don't understand how he's able to cross over to my reality, but he is definitely my Loki with his distinctive backstory as the gods Kokopelli, Raven, Coyote, Tezcatlipoca, Bastet, Seth, Eris, Hermes, and Hephaistos spanning five thousand years of Earth's history, equivalent to one thousand of Asgard's vast age.

My heart ached as we talked about the loss of his mother, Frigga's twin sister, from whom he'd inherited his distinctive looks and black seidhr that gave him the nickname the Black Prince. But it was discussing his murdered wife, Sigyn, killed during the last Elven-Asgardian war that affected me more than I'd anticipated. The pain in those emerald eyes of his struck me with a visceral impact, far harder than when I'd simply written out his history in my character sketch. Not giving him clues as to what his future held had me gritting my teeth, but careful questioning revealed that unlike backstory elements, until I wrote the chapter and sent it to my beta-readers, the future wasn't real for him yet.

After trying to wrap my mind around it all, I return my focus to writing the story my soul insists on telling. I hit the button and the box pops up on my screen, announcing that I've just sent chapter five of *Hidden* to my beta-readers. Stretching my arms over my head, I smile to myself. A new character makes an appearance in this chapter. I fidget in my seat as I can't wait to see what my readers think. I hate waiting. It's like being a kid on Christmas Eve, unable to sit still or sleep, excited, impatient, and hopeful. I need to distract myself from constantly refreshing my profile page, anxious for comment notifications.

Pushing my laptop off my knees and onto the chaise where I do most of my writing, I get up and walk to the kitchen. Now is a good time for a caffeine break and maybe some breakfast. The morning sunlight reflects off the lake and through the large windows, shining on the blue-black granite countertops I'd had installed after my grandmother, my last remaining family member, passed away two years ago. Her death left me well-set financially, but alone in the world.

Hot tea or iced tea? Decisions, decisions.

Something warm would be nice. I rub my hands up and down, gooseflesh rising on my bare arms from the chilly air in the house. It isn't quite cold enough to turn on the gas fireplace, but I don't have the furnace on either. Opening the rich golden brown oak door of the upper cabinet, I take out a canister of my favourite tea, Earl Grey.

A mug? Or brew a full teapot? My gaze flits between the instant hot water tap and my kettle. The little tank under the counter holds enough for a cup or two, or preheating the teapot, but isn't sufficient for both warming the pottery teapot and brewing a pot.

A shiver raising the hair on my neck makes the decision for me.

It's definitely more than a single-cup kind of morning. Setting the metallic blue kettle in the sink to fill, I turn on the tap and bounce on my toes, rubbing my arms as I listen as the tone changes, indicating the kettle is almost full.

After shutting off the water, I lift the heavy kettle and set it on the thick, wooden cutting board at one end of the large center island that divides the kitchen from the family room. Plugging it in and flipping the switch to on, I turn and take a few steps to the fridge. As I reach for the handle, my hair is gripped from behind and I'm tugged back against a hard male body by a powerful arm around my waist. A shocked gasp escapes my lips.

"I am displeased with you, little writer," he growls, his voice menacing as he emphasizes each word.

I squeak as my heart races, my pulse thundering in my ears. Although I'm almost sure he won't hurt me, there is that tiny niggle of doubt that has me frozen in place. Each shallow breath pulls in the scent of wood, orange, and leather.

"What... what's wrong, Loki? I thought you and Shannon enjoyed yourselves at the theatre?" My voice breaks as I try to get the words out past my instinctual flight-or-fight response to having the powerful God of Chaos angry with me.

"Oh, I did. Absolutely. I'm confident she enjoyed it as well, but then she left!" he snarls into my right ear, his breath tickling the sensitive skin of my neck.

I close my eyes, flinching at his tone. I know things are going to happen in the story that will make him angry, upset, and even hurt, but they need to occur. It's essential that I resolve this with him now if I'm to have any chance of surviving the writing of this trilogy. Being the first writer to get strangled by her own character is not on my agenda.

I lick my lips. All the spit has disappeared from my mouth, and I force myself to speak in a firm tone. "I'm sorry, Loki. Events will happen in this story that you won't agree with, but that's why I'm the writer and you're the character. Some things need to happen. You have to trust me and deal with the consequences of the plot I lay out."

With a growl, his teeth clamp down on the right side of my neck at its base, just hard enough for me to feel the sharp pinch. It's such a dominant, animalistic move that I gasp even as my nipples tighten in response.

Releasing my flesh, his tongue licks an achingly slow trail up to my ear, sending shivers down my nape. "I know that but I don't have to like it, now do I? I'll tell you what I do like, though." His voice shifts to a low, sinful purr that floods me with exquisite anticipation. "The way you stood up to me to defend your story. That was hot, my little writer. Very, very sexy." His teeth nip my earlobe. "Of course, that just makes it so much sweeter when I do get your surrender."

Turning me away from the fridge, he moves me forward until my lower body is pinned between the island and him. The hand at my waist delves under my t-shirt to cup my naked breast before tugging the taut nipple, rolling it between his thumb and forefinger.

I whimper at the bolt of lust that spears my core, and his lips stretch into a smile against my neck. He kisses the pulse fluttering madly under his mouth.

"And you will surrender, won't you? Tell me you want me to fuck that tight little cunt of yours with this big, hard cock." He rolls his hips against my ass and the long, rigid length pushes against me like a fiery brand, scorching me through my pyjama bottoms, my sex clenching with need.

Oh my god, I do. I want him, no thoughts whatsoever on denying him. He's a drug I can't get enough of. His scent, his voice... he doesn't even have to touch me and my body heats, readying for his possession, for the pleasure he brings me.

"Yes, Loki," I moan. "Please."

He kisses my neck, again with a lick over my frantic pulse, and releases my hair and breast to yank my shirt over my head. With a hand on my upper back, he slowly pushes my chest down to meet the countertop. I suck in a sharp breath as the cold granite shocks my peaked nipples, instinctively trying to jerk away.

"No, stay like that," he commands, pushing me down onto the icy stone before his hands pull my pyjama bottoms and panties down to mid-thigh, trapping my legs together.

My skin prickles, heat spreading in my abdomen and contrasting with the cold counter as fingertips graze a delicate trail from the base of my neck, down the centre of my back, between the cleft of my ass, to tease lightly across damp, heated flesh.

I squirm, a breathy whimper escaping my lips. God, I love the way he touches me.

"Such a beautiful sight to have you bent over, aching and wet for me. Just one more thing to make the image of your surrender complete." He takes my t-shirt and wraps it around my right wrist. Moving my arm to my lower back, he holds it there as he does something to tie my other wrist to it, pinning both together. "Now that is picture perfect, bound and waiting for whatever I desire."

He's held me in place before, but never tied me. The anticipation of what he'll do next has my pulse pounding and my breath panting.

"You like that, don't you? Being helpless and under my control? Answer me or I won't touch you," he demands in that wicked, purred growl that shivers over my senses.

"Yes, Loki," I moan, wiggling my ass a bit.

He chuckles, a mix of amusement and sinister torment in the sound. Arousal trickles out of my core, and I whimper in frustrated need.

A finger strokes over my folds, delves inside, and finds the flushed bundle of nerves. My hips jerk in reaction and a moan escapes me as the finger flicks back and forth.

"Loki, please," I beg.

I swivel my head to gaze behind at him and a shock runs through me when I spot Thor in the doorway off to the side, concealed from Loki's view by the fridge. While I have numerous characters in my novels, only Loki has visited me in person until now. How is Thor here, too? Have I lost my mind?

Maybe, despite all the evidence, I am dreaming?

Chapter Four

Begging

Shirtless, his impressive physique fully on display, Thor leans his shoulder against the doorjamb, blue eyes filled with a dark lust. Red hair surrounds his strong features and brushes his broad, powerful shoulders. My gaze follows the ridges of muscle down to his tapered waist, then lower. I swallow. There's a sprinkling of red hairs trailing into the now unbuttoned waist of his brown leather pants, lovingly hugging his hips. Unable to stop devouring the sight, I watch as his hand continues unbuttoning his pants, releasing a massive cock. Our eyes meet, and his lips twitch in a sinful half-smile as his fingers begin to stroke.

My core tightens in a helpless spasm, even as a surge of moisture floods Loki's finger. Oh, god. This is not how I envisioned meeting another of my characters. Thor is exactly as I imagined, although I hadn't actually considered how well-endowed he is. But then, his mother Frigga is a fertility goddess.

"What are you thinking, little writer, that you drenched my hand just now? I'm still only teasing you," Loki asks with a curious tilt of his head as I drag my sight away from Thor and look back at him.

My gaze can't help but flicker between the brothers. Cousins by blood, until Loki's mother, Frigga's twin sister, died and Frigga adopted Loki, yet the family resemblance is there in height, muscular build—albeit Thor is larger and stockier—facial expressions, and oh god, cock size.

Between Loki's fingers playing with my clit and the erotic visual of Thor with his large hand wrapped around his cock watching us, I'm squirming.

Loki's eyes narrow and he leans to the left, following my sight line.

"Really, Brother? You had to barge in on us?" Loki says with annoyance.

"Hey, I just followed you, and I'm definitely enjoying the show. Don't stop on my account. Our little writer looks hot as fuck, all helplessly bound as you play with her." Thor's voice is deep and rough with arousal, sending a shiver up my spine.

Loki smirks. "Yes, she does, doesn't she." His eyes narrow, one dark brow rising. "But what makes you think I'm willing to share, Thor? Or that I'm okay with you watching?"

Thor's wicked smile broadens, meeting my gaze with a look full of heat and promise that has me writhing. "Because while you are rightly possessive about Shannon inside the story universe, this is *our* writer in *her* universe. Melody doesn't belong solely to you. She belongs to all of her characters, just as we belong to her." He meets Loki's eyes and cocks his own eyebrow. "Plus, you're a sex god, Loki. Acknowledge you can't resist exploring *every* way to make those pretty lips beg or elicit those delicious moans. You know you want to push her boundaries to figure out what gets her little pussy gushing and cumming over and over. Tell me I'm wrong, Brother."

Loki sighs. "You are aware I don't like to share, but I won't argue with you. Look at how she's soaked and glistening—these pretty pussy lips flushed such a gorgeous rose. She practically came when she saw you watching us, jerking your cock."

Instead of making me self-conscious, the two of them talking about me makes my toes curl. Every inch of me is hyper-aware, my skin prickling with sensation. If you'd told me I'd feel this way even a few weeks ago, I would have called you a liar.

Loki traces his fingertips over me as he talks and finally presses two inside, slowly moving them in and out. "You should have felt how her tiny, little cunt trembled, and I got that without even having my fingers within her at the time. Just listen to her. She'd get a dead man hard."

I'm panting, so aroused I'm quivering and mewling.

Thor steps near, stopping by my left hip next to Loki, but far enough back that I can still see his hand moving up and down his rigid length. Fuck, my mouth waters to taste him, to lick that thick rosy head with its gleaming pearlescent drops welling at the slit. Loki hasn't let me explore or touch him that way, always telling me I'll get a chance later.

"What do you say, Melody? Do you want me watching and jerking my cock as my brother plunders your soaked little pussy?" Thor asks.

My core spasms, clinging to Loki's digits. By the gods, I don't care if this is the best damn delusion I've ever had. It can't stop. Please.

"Fuck, did you see that? She's clamping down on my fingers so tight, I can barely move them. I'd say that's a yes, but we need to hear the words. Answer us, little writer," Loki demands.

"Please! Yes, Loki! God, yes," I agree between breathless moans.

The brothers look at each other and smile. And not nice smiles. Oh no. Instead, these are full of erotic intent, dark satisfaction, and wicked mischief. I can't help but think that means trouble for me, and god, do I want *everything* those smiles imply. A shiver ripples over my body.

"And what about Thor?" Loki's voice has dropped into a low, sinful purr that has heat tightening my core while his fingers continue their slow, teasing strokes in and out. "When I've ravaged you, left you limp and dripping with my scent and seed, do you want his huge cock fucking your little cunt? I don't even know if it will fit, but he'll force it into your tight quim if you need him to. He'll fill you so full, the cum will gush down your thighs when he's done. Do you desire that?"

"Oh my god, yes. Yes, Loki." I buck my hips against his fingers, trying to increase the pace.

His voice drops further as he leans over to whisper in my ear. "Do you want me to watch him take you? Knowing that seeing him fuck your little pussy in front of me will make me so fucking insane that I'll be plotting how to brand your body with my claim, ravishing you so thoroughly that you'll never, ever doubt you belong to me? There will be consequences to sharing your body in my presence. You won't know when or where. I'll let it stew and build, keeping you on edge. Are you *certain* you wish to ignite that fuse?"

"Please... please, Loki. Yes," I moan. I'm not afraid of Loki's possessiveness. It's all sexual dominance and not an attempt to control any other aspects of my life. He's just interested for now... until he finds someone else who intrigues him more. But I'm going to enjoy this fling, even if I have no explanation for his physical presence here, in my world, while it lasts.

The fingers disappear and wider, hotter flesh stretches me, impaling me with slow, relentless force. A long, low moan is pulled from my throat as I adjust to the delicious fullness.

Loki starts grinding in and out in achingly long, slow movements. The friction has me wanting to scream. It's so perfect as my sex clenches and heat shimmers over me.

Hands holding my hips, Loki tilts me so the head of his cock rubs over my G-spot with every measured thrust. I'm having a hard time saying words or making sense of anything as my entire being focuses on the nerves sparking hotter and hotter. Some part of my brain registers the growling coming from Loki as he drives himself in and out of me at his controlled pace, and the sight of Thor's hand stroking his cock, eyes like sapphires, cheeks flushed with rising lust.

"Damn, that is so fucking hot. Make her cum, Loki," Thor demands.

The heat builds and builds until it's an overwhelming wave. Like a dam that's hit its limit and loses structural integrity, I burst, screaming as I buck violently, pinned to the cold counter by Loki's hot body.

Harder and faster now, his hips and thighs smack into my ass with pounding thrusts. I'll be bruised where my legs hit the unyielding granite edge and I don't care. It's totally worth it—proof of his presence later when he's gone—and at the moment, I'm not feeling any pain. I'm flying on endorphins. My entire focus is on the cock hitting so deep inside in a pleasurable stretch that it has me squeezing my inner thighs at the onslaught.

Tingling and quivering, the heat builds again, flaring out from my core to my thighs, to my ass, and up my spine. Before I can prepare for it, it's right there, another cataclysmic orgasm that tears through me, shakes me, and wrings me out.

Within a few thrusts, as I continue to spasm with the waves of my climax, Loki's growled shout echoes throughout the room. He pulses, filling me with his last few strokes before he stops moving, sunk to the hilt, and I sense the hot flood.

He's breathing heavily, a match to my wheezing. My heart is a drumbeat in my ears. I don't even realize I've closed my eyes at the point of climax until I open them to see Thor. A jolt goes through me as he uses his thumb to spread glistening pre-cum over the head of his massive cock.

Chapter Five

Wisdom Is Overrated

Loki chuckles. "Our little writer just recovered enough to see the monster you are going to attempt to shove inside this hot, wet cunt and squeezed so hard she's got a death grip around me." He leans over to brush the hair off my face, kissing my neck on the thudding pulse as he purrs in my ear. "Relax those tight little pussy muscles, darling, unless you want my brother to split you in two. Or have you changed your mind?"

Consciously, I try to relax. I am both excited and a bit nervous. My core still throbs with Loki inside me. Whereas his cock stretches me, he's the width of my arm just above my wrist. Thor isn't longer, but his cock is closer to the width of my forearm, near my elbow. It's intimidating and arousing as hell.

"Answer me, little one. I need to hear you want this," Loki demands with a growl in my ear.

"Yes, Loki," I gasp out between panted breaths. Even as he pushes me to try new things, Loki still checks to make sure it's something I want. It's an aspect of him I appreciate, despite it not being something I'd created in my character sketch of him. If my mind wasn't so distracted, I'd try to think about that more.

But not now. No, now my eyes are fixed on Thor.

Pushing himself up, Loki caresses his hand down my back, sending a shiver over my skin. "Do you need me to adjust your arms? They haven't gone numb?"

"They're good," I answer, cherishing the way Loki always takes the time to ensure I'm never in real pain or distress.

Holding my hips, Loki slowly draws out of me with a groan. He's still hard, despite his orgasm. Perks of being a sex god, as based on the experiences of this last week, I know he would have continued if Thor wasn't here. I writhe at the erotic, wet sound as he slides free of my body.

The brothers swap places. Thor's larger hands squeeze my ass, then caress up my sides with widespread fingertips. The warm, firm touch is bold, with prickles of sensation flaring across my flesh.

"I want to explore you, taste and touch you, but I'm so fucking hot for you, I don't have the patience right now," he tells me in a deep rumble of sound.

His thick cock nestles against my wet core, tantalizingly close, as he rolls his hips against my ass. He teases me, sliding it back and forth. My eyes almost roll back in my head every time he rubs over my clit and lightning flares through my sex.

But that's all he does. Tease me.

"If you don't stop teasing me and shove that giant cock in my pussy right now, I'm going to get angry," I snarl after several minutes have passed.

Loki's eyes meet mine, and he smirks. "You better do it, Brother. She means business."

I twist my head to see Thor's expression, and he's smiling. "She gets feisty for such a small person. I like it."

I'm about to growl at him when I'm distracted by the painful stretch in my core. It has me panting as he slowly pushes the head inside.

"*Fuck!* She is so damn tiny," Thor groans.

"I'm not tiny. You are fucking huge!" I retort. God, why didn't I imagine him a bit smaller? Is this my fault? Maybe my character sketches need to be more... specified.

Thor has paused with just the head of his cock inside, and although there's a definite bite of pain to the stretch, I relax into it after a minute, letting my uneven breaths calm.

All at once, I shove back onto him in a hard surge, gasping as he's fully seated with his hips tight to my ass. Pleasure, with a sharp bite of pain, blasts straight up my spine and greys my vision for a few seconds.

"*Fucking crazy*! I can't believe you just did that," Thor shouts as he groans loudly.

His length throbs against my inner walls and the sensation sends more sparking ripples shooting up my nerve endings. I tighten, squeezing him in reaction.

"You are going to make me cum like a randy teen with his first woman if you don't stop that." Thor smacks my ass with a sharp crack and my hips jerk.

I yelp at the initial flash of pain, then moan as the heat settles deeper into my core.

"Did you see that, Loki? Looks like we've found something else that gets our little writer wet and writhing."

A slow smile stretches Loki's lips as he meets my wide gaze, and I know he's not going to forget.

"I did, indeed, take note of that. Now stop playing and fuck our girl like you mean it. She's managed to accommodate your monster cock. Make good use of it and make her cum," Loki demands.

He hasn't finished speaking when Thor starts to move, and my eyes flutter closed. The pleasure is overwhelming, even at the slow, careful pace he's setting. Every stroke sends a sparking flare expanding out from my abdomen.

I know he'll bring me to orgasm like this, but I'm impatient. Damn it, I crave it now. I shove back onto him, meeting his thrusts.

"Harder Thor. I need harder," I whimper.

Loki nods, and soon, Thor's plunging in and out at a tempo that has me keening as the pleasure becomes exquisitely on the border of pain. It's incredibly intense, and my entire pelvis tingles with pleasurable sparks in a fast, onrushing storm.

One minute, the feeling is building, and the next, I'm writhing as it bursts over me in a thunderous tempest.

Thor doesn't stop. He doesn't even slow down. He fucks me right through the ripples of my orgasm with strong, sure strokes. As his hips bottom out against my ass on each thrust, he groans.

Building rapidly again with so many nerve endings singing, shooting flares spark up my spine in progressively brighter bursts that pop with each impact of Thor's cock against my cervix. My feet leave the floor as he lifts my hips, changing the angle of his thrusts to bump that deep, pleasurable spot behind my cervix.

Squirming, bucking, trembling in his hands, I'm unable to stay still, driven mad by the sparking bubbles that keep expanding. I'm begging, but I don't even know what I'm asking for.

Thor pulls my upper body off the counter, lifting me back against his chest as he continues to plunge in and out, rubbing over my G-spot while still hitting that spot deep inside. I'm trembling, wound taut like a bowstring ready to fire, the overwhelming lightning forking out from my core.

Fingers smack my clit and pinch a nipple in a coordinated attack and I detonate in a violent starburst, electricity searing through me, white light exploding in my brain, blanking out all thought.

It takes me a moment to realize I've passed out for a few seconds, missing time.

When I can think again, Thor groans, the hot gush of his seed filling me with the last few twitches of his cock. He's still holding me up against his chest. One hand cradles my breast, tugging on the nipple and another cups my mound, fingers slowly stroking over my clit. It's too sensitive, but I'm unable to squirm away with my hands pinned between our bodies.

Lungs heaving, I look over and meet Loki's eyes. His pupils are blown wide, glittering with lust as he wipes cum off the counter beside me. Watching me clearly pushed him to a second orgasm. I can't help but be disappointed that I missed seeing him lose control. He tucks his still-rigid cock into his pants and steps over to me, stopping Thor's hand on my clit.

"Too much?" Loki asks, and I nod.

Gently, Thor lays me back down on the counter, and Loki unties my wrists. He brings each arm forward, massaging the muscles until I'm braced on my forearms. My pulse still pounds, and I'm trying to catch my breath.

Carefully, Thor pulls out his softening cock. A gush of cum drips down my thighs in a hotly erotic flood.

"Oh god," I moan, grateful for the counter's support to hold me up. Loki runs the tap, wetting a dishcloth with hot water.

Bending, Thor tugs my damp pyjama bottoms and panties down my trembling limbs and off. Loki wipes my inner thighs and core with gentle swirls of the cloth, before rinsing it in the sink and cleaning me again.

"Do you want a shower or right to bed for a nap?" asks Thor.

"My legs are like wet noodles. I don't think I can walk right now," I giggle, sounding pleasure-drunk.

"Bed, then. You need your rest, little human."

Thor scoops me up in his arms, and I lean my head against his chest, listening to his heartbeat—a steady, strong rhythm as he carries me upstairs to my bedroom. In his powerful arms, I feel petite in a way I never have before. At five foot seven and decidedly curvy, I'm no lightweight and taller than most Canadian women, yet both brothers top me by more than half a foot. Thor doesn't strain at carrying my weight, and I can't help but trace the firm curves of his pectorals with my fingertips. He smiles down at me, satisfied eyes gleaming.

Loki pulls back my covers and moves the pillow into place before stepping out of the way. Thor lays me down, pulls up the blankets and kisses me lightly.

"I'll see you again, Melody," Thor says, brushing his hand over my hair.

Loki sits down on the side of the bed after Thor moves away. He purrs, leaning down to my ear, "Rest and recover, little writer. You are going to need it."

The remembered dark promise is in his eyes as my lids start drooping, and there is a gentle press of his lips on mine. God, if this is all a dream, please don't wake me. Lethargy pulls at my thoughts. Despite the delicious soreness between my thighs, I sink into the bed, my muscles relaxed, and I'm asleep before they disappear.

CHAPTER SIX

Embrace The Chaos

I'm shaking my head at myself. It was an impulsive decision my characters from two different fictional universes to get together for a Halloween party at my place, here in the real world... or at least what I consider the real world. Since Thor's visit last week, more of my characters have popped into my reality. It's almost like Loki has opened some kind of door and now the rest can come through.

However, unlike those two Asgardian gods, my other characters share a meal, talk, drink tea, or walk on my beach with me. No demands for a special agreement between us. No hanky-panky. No mind-melting sex that leaves me boneless and satiated.

I've only seen Loki twice in the last week since his brother made his appearance. His words still prey on my mind, but he hasn't said anything further. He hasn't acted on his threat... yet.

A wave of gooseflesh travels down my back, and I push away the shiver of arousal thinking of Loki always gives me. I finish connecting the hook-eye clasps on the corset for the old theatre costume dress from a Victorian-era play. Every time my characters visit, I learn something new about them. I've noticed that when they visit me here, they retain their personalities and traits I've given them, but make their own choices. They have the freedom to act of their own free will, unlike in their fictional universe, where I dictate everything that happens to them and how they react.

It's why I've invited them all at once. It's Halloween. Why not have a costume party? I'm curious to find out what they'll pick when I don't choose for them.

Fortunately, my dress isn't historically accurate, allowing me to avoid the enormous weight of material or tons of skirt layers. I do still have to pick up the long skirt to walk up or down stairs so I don't fall on my ass or break my neck, but that's doable.

But perhaps I spoke too soon.

As I descend the stairs from my bedroom, a knock at my front door startles me, and I stumble, missing the bottom step as the door opens.

Kara catches me with her fast reflexes. "Whoa there, Melody. Have you been into the ale already?" she asks with a laugh.

"Thank you! No, I'm just not used to wearing a floor-length skirt. I don't know how women back then dealt with this all the time."

Mist snorts and closes the door behind her. "It becomes second nature. I don't miss it though, because wow, hygiene was bad. People smelled!"

I wrinkle my nose. "Sounds gross."

Kara nods. "It was. Speaking of, where do you want the ale?"

"In the fridge." I gesture to the stainless steel appliance as we walk around the corner and into the kitchen. "So, let me guess…" I take in Kara's fake fangs, black shirt, pants, boots, and trench coat, her lips blood-red, and her curly red hair piled up on her head. "Vampire?"

She smirks. "Yeah, I know. Not that original, but it's a classic for a reason. And Hecate's empousai are all female, unlike the Midgardian vampires." She pops the top off of a dark bottle of ale and offers it to me.

"Is that Asgardian?" I ask.

"Of course."

Shaking my head, I laugh. "Yeah, I'll pass. Not only do I lack your immortal stamina, but I also don't want to spend the party in a drunken stupor, or discover I'm an accidental goddess."

Kara smirks. "Fair enough."

Mist swipes the open bottle from her, swigging half of it back. "Okay, so guess my costume!"

Her usual multi-tonal blue hair is covered by a shaggy orange wig, styled just below her chin. She's dressed in a white crop top, gold and black capris, with orange holey suspenders crossing between her legs and around her ribs on the side.

"It's quite the look, but I like that movie. Leeloo from the *Fifth Element*!" I grin when she pouts.

"That's a great movie!" says a voice from behind me.

Turning, my next two visitors have arrived, joining us in the kitchen. "Hey, Lynn. Hi, Paula. Totally agree. This is Mist, a Valkyrie from Asgard. Kara, the vampire, is also a Valkyrie. Lynn is a human scientist with Agriculture Canada. Lynn, I see you chose Harley Quinn for your costume?"

Lynn laughs, flipping her coloured pigtails with a hand as she shares an amused glance with Paula. "Emily chose it for me. She wanted to come, but you said adults only."

"You're a scientist, too?" Shannon arrives, stepping through the open doorway in what appears to be a wizard costume influenced by Harry Potter and introduces herself to Lynn.

The two of them head off to one of the couches to chat, so I turn to introduce Paula to Mist and Kara. A laugh bursts out of me when I take in her suit and the FBI name badge hanging from her jacket. The costume effortlessly matches her auburn, chin-length hair as if made for her. "Paula, who is impersonating Agent Scully from *The X-files*, is an officer with the Canadian Security Intelligence Agency. That means she's a spook, a spy."

Paula winks at the two Valkyrie, then attempts to look innocent when I raise an eyebrow.

"Now, that sounds like an interesting job," Kara tells Paula as she hands her an ale, and they wander away to sit at another couch to chat.

My mouth opens, then closes, as I turn to Mist. "Should I warn Lynn and Paula about the ale?"

Mist grins and waves a dismissive hand. "Nah. It doesn't exist in their world, right? Let them have some fun."

"What world would that be?" James asks as he steps up to wrap me in his arms, giving me a warm hug, with Matt right beside him.

"Asgard," I tell him, and his eyes widen.

"Really? Like the superhero movies?" he asks, releasing me.

"Not really. Asgard's a planet, not a weird flat landmass with water falling off the side. How about I introduce you to Shannon? She's chatting with Lynn. Shannon is a fellow Canadian and can explain her universe to you." Taking James by the hand, I walk over to where Shannon and Lynn are talking. "Shannon, this is Canadian Prime Minister James Hunter. James, Shannon is an ecology professor at Victoria Charles University."

And an immortal Elven goddess, but she doesn't know that yet. I bite my lip, thinking about that upcoming reveal in *Hidden*. She's in for quite the ride to discover her powers.

As I walk away, I overhear Shannon compliment James on his pirate costume. Looking around for Matt, I see Mist has already introduced herself to him, and they're sitting by the fireplace. I'm amused to see James' protection detail security chief—the clean-cut, usually impeccably dressed Royal Canadian Mounted Police Superintendent—in a badass biker costume. Black leather encases his tall, muscular form. Together with his black hair and neatly trimmed beard, it makes for a good look. Very hot.

Only Thor and Loki have yet to arrive. Somehow, it doesn't surprise me that they'll be making an entrance. I have no doubt I'll know when they arrive.

Neither Asgardian god is inconspicuous in the least.

CHAPTER SEVEN

Their Pitch

I watch the three sets of conversations for a while and it strikes me that when visiting me here, my characters are like a group of actors getting together. They have the same personalities I created for them, but they don't necessarily retain the emotional connections from within their storyline. Instead, each is limited in their knowledge of the future to what I've written so far.

Still, I would expect Lynn and James to flirt. But no, Lynn and Shannon are deep in a discussion of some scientific topic, and James has moved to join Kara and Paula.

It makes me wonder. What happens to them when I revise something? Is it like the movie *The Matrix*, where their universe glitches and resets, but they don't notice? And how do they know so much backstory detail I haven't necessarily created yet? It's a freaky paranormal, multiverse mind-bender for sure that I can't even begin to try to understand.

Shaking my head, I walk into the kitchen and remove trays of food from the fridge that I'd prepared earlier in the day. We're definitely going to need them. Mist and Matt are pouring and passing around shots of tequila or Asgardian mead. Either Mist is rubbing off on him, or Matt has a hidden bad-boy side I haven't yet explored in his character.

Maybe I'll use that aspect for a sequel to the *Gallows Tree Conspiracy*.

"Hey Paula, crank up that music!" Lynn shouts, and Shannon whoops beside her. The driving beat of dance music vibrates throughout the house.

I grin to myself as I unwrap the trays, swivelling my hips back and forth to the beat. My house is usually so quiet, with just me rattling around in it. I don't even have a pet. The recent weeks of visitors have made for a distinct change. It's fun to have company livening it up. Clearly, the shots are having the desired effect as everyone lets loose.

An arm wraps around my shoulder as another clasps my waist from opposite sides, two large bodies pressing in against me, stilling my movements, and trapping me against the island.

"Is it fate we once again find our little writer pinned against this very convenient island? It really is the perfect height and very sturdy for a repeat engagement," a voice purrs.

Instant shivers of awareness turn my skin to goosebumps.

I twist to look at Loki, his eyes dark with intimate knowledge as one side of his mouth twitches up into a half smile. My pulse picks up, throbbing in my veins as my breath shortens. He's wearing a gentleman's regency-era suit, complete with trousers tucked into hessian boots, cravat, waistcoat, and jacket with tails. Historical or not, men's formal wear is incredibly sexy on him.

He looks absolutely amazing.

Like the tall, dark, and handsome hero from one of those bodice-ripper stories. Or an even hotter version of Colin Firth's Mister Darcy. Damn. I didn't think that was possible, and I do love watching *Pride and Prejudice* at least once a year.

Distracted by his mouth-watering appearance, it takes me a few minutes to realize that Loki's eyes are also looking me over, lingering on my heaving breasts in the constricting corset, his smile growing as his gaze returns to mine.

"You'd think she *wants* us to bend her over, toss up these skirts, and fuck her until she can't walk again. Did you *see* how her sexy little ass was moving when we arrived? What do you suppose she's wearing under there, Brother?" an amused deep rumble says from my other side. "Want to bet on whether it's historically accurate?"

Ripping myself from Loki's magnetic gaze, I turn to Thor. His blue eyes are heated, but playful, with a sensual grin on his face. He winks as our gaze meets, and like Loki, he takes his time perusing my form, letting me know with his expression that he likes what he sees.

I do the same, taking in his desert sultan outfit that gives the impression he's eying me as an addition to his harem.

"We could very easily find out," Loki suggests, his hand moving from my waist down onto my ass.

My head whips back to Loki, my mouth dropping open in shock.

"To hell with food. I want to eat her. How long do you think it would take for everyone to notice we're fucking her brains out?" Thor wonders.

"Not long, unless we put that moaning mouth of hers to good use." Loki smirks as I let out a squeak.

My pulse flutters in my veins, with heat pooling in my core in a confusing mix of intensely aroused and shocked at the suggestion. And he can see it, damn him. He runs a fingertip over my lower lip, tugging on it, before sliding it deliberately into my mouth. I bite down, just letting him feel my teeth, and he pulls it out, his eyes narrowing in warning.

"Stop getting our writer all hot and bothered. Loki doesn't share, so there's no way you two are going to spread her on the counter and..."

Thor, Loki, and I all look at Mist, whose expression goes from eye-rolling sarcasm to widening surprise, followed closely by lips curving in amusement.

"Holy Norns!" She laughs, and my cheeks flush fiery red. "Oh, to be a fly on the wall when *that* happened!"

I cover my face, thoroughly embarrassed.

"Mist!" growls Thor, even as Loki turns my face into his chest. I'm not ashamed, but I hadn't planned on announcing it.

Loki puts his fingers under my chin, tilting my head up to look at him. "Are you okay?"

That both of them instantly switch from teasing to defending me, taking care of my feelings, ignites a warm glow inside me.

I give Loki a small smile. "I'm just embarrassed at having it announced. But I don't regret it for even a microsecond, if that's what you're worried about."

He smiles in approval, and his fingers caress my cheek. "I knew you were made of sterner stuff. After all, you write all of us, including this fool." He tilts his head towards Mist.

She's smiling but also fidgeting. "I didn't mean to embarrass you. Frankly, I'm in awe and totally jealous. Not of these two, because eww, they are like my brothers, but to use a line you wrote, you are a badass, Melody. I hope that if I get any sex scenes in the future—not that I'm trying to tell you what to write—but I'd appreciate you doing the research with whomever you'd be hooking me up with to ensure it's great." She gives me a wink and wiggles her blue eyebrows.

I cock my head and blink, wondering if I've heard her right. "Did you just tell me you'd like me to have sex with whatever character I might pair you with for a sex scene... because you want me to ensure the sex is great?"

Chapter Eight

It's For Research

"If you write sex scenes for me, I want the sex to be *amazing*! So, yes, yes I do," she says enthusiastically, nodding her head.

Thor grins and pumps his fist in the air. "Good. That means I get to have sex in the story at some point, since you are doing research with me."

Loki snorts a laugh, and I cover my face with my hand, groaning.

"I know I've appreciated the research you are doing so far!" Shannon yells, joining the conversation. "Fuck Loki some more, okay? I want to try new things!"

"Oh my god," I groan louder, and Loki bites his lip, trying to hold in the amusement that is making his eyes tear up. "Loki!" I punch him in the arm, and he chuckles.

Shannon and Lynn whisper back and forth a few times before she shouts, "Hey, you're going to fuck James, right?

Because it sure seems like we are headed that way, and I want amazing sex, too!"

James stands, leaving his conversation with Paula, Kara, and Matt, and coming over to join us. "Who are the sultan and Regency gentlemen?" he inquires.

"Thor and Loki," Mist tells him, pointing to each of them. "Asgardian gods, this is James Hunter, Canadian Prime Minister."

James leans across the island and shakes their hands. "Lynn said something about us having sex? Did I hear that right?" he asks me, his blue eyes flaring with interest even as his mouth twitches in an amused smile.

"Lynn wants Melody to have sex with you, so when she writes sex scenes between the two of you, she'll know your quirks and be able to write amazing scenes," Thor explains, chuckling.

With a whimper, I put my head down on the counter, my hands over my ears. My face cannot get any redder. I can't *believe* we are having this conversation. Why did I invite my characters all together? What the hell was I thinking?

"You should seduce our little writer," Loki recommends. "She probably won't call on you of her own volition, but if you want her to write sex scenes for you, definitely seduce her. Way better scenes for you and Lynn both."

I lift my head and glare at Loki. "*Stop* pimping me out."

His eyes glitter, meeting my gaze with a slight quirk on his lips. He's not intimidated in the least by my ire, damn it.

"I wouldn't dream of taking advantage of you or overstepping where I'm not wanted, Melody," James says, a hint of hurt in his tone.

"You. Shut it. Now!" I snap, pointing at Loki, who puts his hands up in surrender despite the mischief lurking in his eyes. He makes a zipping motion with his fingers over his lips. Right. Like I'm going to fall for that fake wide-eyed, innocent look. He hasn't been innocent in hundreds of years. Fucker.

I push past a still chuckling Thor, poking him in the chest with a fingertip and trying to not notice when the unyielding muscle bends my finger, to walk around the island until I reach James. Sliding one hand into his dark hair, I tilt his head down. I look up into his blue eyes, seeing a little confusion, uncertainty, and hurt. A sinking sensation hits my gut, and I wince.

"I am not rejecting you, James. Not at all. Yes, I write much better scenes between characters when I've researched the ins and outs of each of you."

A muffled laugh comes from my left, and I close my eyes to try to ignore it.

Giving an annoyed huff at my inadvertent slip of the tongue, I meet his gaze again and continue, "As much as it pains me, because I am *never* going to hear the end of it once I say this, but Loki's not wrong."

I shift to glare at Loki, and he winks and blows me a kiss. It makes me roll my eyes, but I can't keep the little smile from my face. I turn back to James. "He's a royal pain in my ass—"

"Not literally, because I haven't fucked that ass yet, but I will!" Loki interjects.

There are a few snorts, coughs, and chuckles at that, and I cover my face with my hand for a second, biting my lip, and trying to not laugh. God, he just really can't help himself.

Lowering my arm, I try again. After a slow exhale, I look up at James. "As I was saying, he knows what he's talking about…"

There are a few more snickers around the room.

When did someone shut off the music, and when did all the conversation stop so everyone can listen to every word that I'm saying? Fuck. You could hear a bloody pin drop in here.

"Oh my god, knock it off all of you!" I say, slapping the granite counter with a palm.

"You called?" Loki asks.

This time, even James laughs as he pulls me in for a tight hug, arms around my waist. Humour lights up his eyes. "He must keep you on your toes. And I understand what you are trying to say. Consider this your warning, then, that I'm going to take his advice at some point." He kisses me lightly with a brief brush of lips, lifting a hand to caress my cheek, then lets me go with a soft smile.

I nod and return his smile.

"On her toes, on her back, on her stomach, bent over the counter…" Loki starts listing, ticking each off on his fingers.

Stomping around the island, I slap my hand over Loki's mouth to get him to stop talking while everyone laughs.

He pulls my hand away, dips me in his arms, and proceeds to kiss me completely senseless.

No, my life hasn't become complicated. Not at all.

57

Delayed Gratification

Episode Two Description

The trickster God of Chaos enjoys toying with me, his writer, but he has more surprises hidden behind those wicked emerald eyes than even I expected.

***

Every writer says their fictional characters talk to them. Mine jumped through the fabric of reality and offered a deal I couldn't refuse. What single woman wouldn't take advantage of the sinfully hot lessons Asgard's sexy Dark Prince wants to teach? He teases, taunts, and hates to share me. But then he left... two weeks without so much as a peep.

Do I move on? Would you?

Chapter Nine

Lakeside Company

The water is the perfect temperature, steam rising into the early December air, as I sink into the depths of the twelve-person hot tub nestled at the edge of the back deck. Grandmother's indulgence—she'd claimed she needed the size to hold meetings of her book club so they could relax their old bones. But like me, I think she just loved the water and wanted to enjoy it year-round. Either way, it is exactly what I need this evening. While I'd had a successful day of writing, after that many hours hunched over my laptop, my brain and body crave the break.

With the jets and house lights off, I float on my back and gaze up at the stars. It's a peaceful night with only a light breeze to barely stir the water's surface and chill my exposed front. Little ripples flow away from me as I flutter my fingers, keeping me from the tub's edges. The hoot of an owl echoes across the lake.

A voice calls out something, but the words are muffled by the burbling water. Lifting my head, I look around. A man's silhouette is in the darkened yard, but his features are obscured. "Sorry? I couldn't hear with my ears underwater."

"How is the water?" asks a familiar, pleasing baritone.

"James?"

"Yes."

My heart gives an extra fast thump as I scan for others. His protection detail is missing. James never visits without at least Matt, his security chief, accompanying him. "It's perfect. You should join me."

Although, now that I consider it, as long as nothing happens to me, he can't be at risk in my world because my writing would bring him to life in the fictional universe, regardless.

Wouldn't it?

I blow out a breath. Trying to understand how my characters jump multiverses to visit me makes my head spin. These last two months, since Loki exploded into my reality and opened the door to my other characters, have been both crazy and some of the best of my life.

James strolls over the grass, tosses his jacket and t-shirt on the deck, toes off his shoes and socks, and shucks his pants. The clink of his belt echoes as it hits a metal brace on the wooden boards. In his dark boxer briefs contrasting against his paler skin, he climbs the stairs, then descends into the depths.

I'm floating on the far side as I watch him approach through the waist-deep water. He ducks under, then emerges, swiping sodden ebony locks out of his eyes. He's close enough now that his smile gleams in the moonlight, highlighting the dark stubble on his strong jaw with the divot in his chin.

"Good evening, Right Honourable Prime Minister," I say with a cheeky grin. "You are looking parliament ready in your almost birthday suit."

His black eyebrows shoot up and amusement stretches his full lips. Reaching out an arm, he snags my foot, using it to pull me closer. "Sassy writer. You are lacking in respect for your nation's leader."

Hmm... is he finally taking Loki's suggestion? It's the first time he's visited since the Halloween party. My pulse quickens. "And what are you going to do about it, *Sir*?" I ask a little breathlessly.

Parting my thighs, he pulls my hips down into the heated water and tugs my core tight to his well-defined stomach as he sinks us into the deep centre of the hot tub. I wrap my legs around him. His skin is a warm contrast with the cool air. With his spread fingers on my lower back, I hook my hands behind his neck. The sprinkle of midnight hairs on his firm chest tickles me in a sensuous stroke, and I brush my breasts back and forth, barely close enough to feel him, but not enough to press against his muscular torso.

His voice drops into a low, seductive caress. "That depends, Melody. Are you going to tease me with your bewitching little body the way you had Lynn do, or will you let me actually fuck you?"

My lips part in a mock gasp, even as a thrill of arousal zips along my nerve endings. "Such language! I'm shocked, Sir! What would your voters think?"

He growls, and it rumbles in his chest. "That you are a teasing minx in need of a good, hard fucking. Give me an answer, woman. I'm tempted to tear that suit right off you." Darkening with desire, the pupils swallow his blue irises as he contemplates the tiny black bikini doing a poor job of hiding my taut nipples a few inches below the water's surface.

Eyes locked on him, I slowly raise my mouth to his, stopping just before we touch. "Rip it off, Sir," I whisper.

Closing the distance, his lips ravage mine in a passionate frenzy of caressing tongues and biting nips, with one hand behind my head holding me to him. My hands wander over his broad shoulders, exploring the ridges and valleys of his fit form and the scars from the explosion that almost took his life in Afghanistan even as he plunders my mouth. I can't get enough of touching him.

He lifts me higher out of the water, tilting my upper body backwards so he can kiss and lick his way down my neck. His tongue traces and captures droplets trickling down my skin. I shiver in reaction.

"You like that, don't you?" he asks, between sweeping licks.

"Yes. Yes, I do," I breathe in a light moan. My nipples ache, and I arch my back, pushing them up at him.

With his eyes on mine, he hooks one hand in the centre of my bikini top between my breasts and snaps the cups apart in a sharp yank. He looks down and smiles, a look of pure masculine admiration. I strain towards him. I need his hot, wet mouth and tongue on me.

"What is it you want, Melody?" he asks in a sensual growl.

The small breeze tightens my nipples further, sensiting them to the lightest stroke. It's a cool caress over my flesh, but I crave his heat. Loki has been teaching me to be bold, to be confident and free to ask for what I desire.

"Please, Sir. Please suck my breasts," I whimper.

James groans and lowers his head, swirling his tongue around them, then pulls back and blows icy air over my wet peaks. Goosebumps shiver over my skin as I squirm against him.

Licking over them again, he teases me until I whine, then sucks them into his mouth. The warmth and wetness surround me with each hard draw, echoing a surge of slick heat in my core.

"Please James, don't stop," I beg. My hands bury into his thick hair, tugging him closer. Every suckling pull sends a stab of arousal spreading and expanding from my sex.

He groans as I grind against the firm ridges of his stomach, trying to add friction to the pulsing in my body from his clever mouth drawing on my nipples. My writhing turns frantic as he brings me higher.

"God! Please, don't stop! Please, god!" I beg, my voice rising with my desperate passion. Surely the water is boiling around us as the heat builds to overwhelming.

His teeth bite while his thumb and forefinger pinch another wet nipple, driving me over the edge. I scream, bucking against his body as the orgasm overwhelms me in a fiery burst.

The sensory overload leaves me shaking, gasping for desperately needed air, when the firmness of the wooden deck surrounding the hot tub presses against my naked back. I hadn't noticed him moving us through the water.

"I've got to taste you," he groans, pulling my hips up towards his head and lifting my legs over his shoulders. He tugs my bikini bottoms to the side, out of the way, as he widens my thighs and lowers his mouth.

The first strokes feather over my clit, driving me crazy with little electric shocks. My hands scramble for something, anything to cling to, finding the rough edge of the deck boards with my fingertips.

His tongue sweeps across me aggressively, and then he nips the sensitive bundle of nerves before flicking the surrounding hood.

"James!" Trembling uncontrollably, my hips jerk at the sharp bolts of sensation sparking up my spine with his repeated strokes.

He hums, vibrating his mouth against my clit as he plunges two fingers into my drenched pussy.

"*James!*" I shriek as the fast orgasm explodes out from my centre and shakes my body.

He groans, "More. That was so fucking beautiful. Give me more."

His curling digits find the most sensitive spot inside me as he learns what I like based on the intensity of my moans and the writhing of my hips. The tension rises, and soon, I'm pleading as he brings me to the edge, then backs off, only to build me up again. I can't help but wonder if he's been somehow talking with Loki, or if this is an innate dominant masculine trait they share to make me lose my mind.

"Please.... Please, James... I can't take anymore... I need you inside me," I beg.

"Not yet." He scoops me up off the edge of the hot tub and deck and into his arms.

"What... why?" Blinking, I look up at him. My flesh buzzes like an electrical wire. Stark arousal has scrambled my thought processes.

"Because I have an idea to drive this little body of yours insane." His voice holds wicked intent as he tugs my bikini bottoms off my legs.

"But you are already making me crazy! Spontaneous combustion is a serious risk right now," I wail, grinding against him.

He laughs as he sets me aside to shed his boxer briefs and deflects my hands as I reach for his gorgeous stiff cock. Sinking us into the heated water, with my ass in his lap, I expect him to impale me on that hard length. Instead, he holds me in place with a powerful arm around my waist while his fingers search the hot tub walls.

"What are you doing?" I ask, squirming against the tempting ridge.

"Looking for... ah ha. Found it. Perfect." He doesn't explain further and sets me on my knees on a seat, facing the outer edge. Positioning himself in the centre of the jacuzzi, with a hand splayed on my lower abdomen, he glides his cock against my entrance.

I squirm, tilting my hips and trying to drive him into my aching core. Whatever he's planning, I'm done waiting. I must have him before I go insane.

"Eager, aren't you? Impatient little minx." His tone is amused as he plants kisses along my neck.

"Will you please fuck me already?" I demand in frustration.

He chuckles, then plunges inside in one hard thrust, sheathing himself.

"*Oh my god!*" The intense fullness has my inner walls twitching, clenching around the steely length. Not as thick as Loki, James is still more than enough.

He tenses, holding himself rigid. Teeth gritted, he groans. "Holy fuck... so damn good."

He withdraws, leaving only the tip inside, then fills me again completely.

"Harder... please, harder," I beg, pushing back towards him.

He snaps his hips faster, nibbling on my neck as his thrusts intensify. I don't realize he's pressing me forward in the seat until a hard stream of water feathers over the junction of my thighs.

"Oh god," I moan as the water pressure starts to bubble over my folds.

James' hand moves down from my lower abdomen to part my sex with his fingers, spreading me wide as he nudges us closer to the jet. Each thrust of his hips drives my core closer to the pulsing water as his cock plunges in and out.

At first, it's a tickle, swirling over my sensitive nub.

He pushes me forward, and it's a rhythmic, throbbing pulse that has me shuddering.

Closer still and the watery blast hammers my clit like a runaway freight train.

"Oh my god! Holy shit! Fuck. *Oh god!*" I'm babbling words that grow progressively louder as I buck uncontrollably. The sensation is so overwhelming I'm not sure if I'm trying to move toward the jet or to escape it. Violent tremors expand in my thighs and abdomen, and I know this orgasm will detonate like a dynamite blast at a rock quarry.

James groans in my ear, his body stiffening behind me.

"Cum for me," he demands, pushing me flush with jet and its punishing aggressive pulse.

I explode.

"Oh my god!"

A shockwave sears up my spine to blow out the top of my head. I contract around his cock in savage waves. I can barely hear his growled shout through the thundering in my ears.

It's too much. Too strong. I can't take it, can't take anymore.

I shove back against him, desperately trying to escape the relentless pounding of the jet against my over-sensitized clit. Seeming to understand, James turns us away from it, and my muscles sag, relaxing into the cresting waves of orgasm that continue to flow over me. The slightest movement cascades ripples of pleasurable aftershocks through our joined bodies.

His head on my shoulder, our breathing eventually normalizes.

"Damn. You feel so good in my arms, it should be criminal." Even his whispered comment sends shivers down my body, and I squeeze around him, drawing a groan as additional waves shake me.

James caresses my cheek with featherlight fingertips before gently lifting me off him, setting off another storm of trembling inside me. He holds me tenderly in his lap, my face pressed against his chest until it stops.

"That was... I don't even know how to describe it." I sound drunk, my words slurring.

With a hand on my chin, he tilts my head up and kisses me softly. "Let's get you dried off and tucked into bed before you fall asleep here in the water."

My knees collapse when I attempt to stand. James chuckles and sweeps me into his arms as he strides up the deck, into the kitchen, up the stairs, and into my bedroom. Getting a towel from my bathroom, he insists on drying me before I pull on the t-shirt I wear as a nightshirt and panties.

As I'm dressing for bed, he dries himself, wrapping the towel around his waist.

"I'll go grab my clothes from outside before I head out." Meeting my gaze, he pulls me over for a lingering kiss that scatters my senses. He draws back, but not before I am clinging to him for support.

He smiles and kisses my nose.

"Into bed, Melody. Sleep well."

Lips curving, I watch him walk out of my bedroom, shutting the door quietly behind him. My eyes close, relaxing into the softness of my bedding, when a familiar purring growl says, "James did a thorough job of seducing you."

CHAPTER TEN

You Called?

With my breath catching in a gasp and eyelids flashing open, I spot Loki leaning against the doorway to my walk-in closet. His emerald gaze narrows, and I sense a hint of censure in the way his lips press together, unsmiling.

My heart beats a rapid tattoo in my chest as a tendril of alarm chases away my euphoria.

"But you knew he would at some point. You even told him to," I answer cautiously, wondering at his mood. "You don't own me, Loki. It's not like we are dating or monogamous."

He slowly straightens at my words, then prowls over to me, a lethal panther stalking his prey that sends a shiver up my spine.

"I know I don't. You are *free* to share this sexy little body with whomever you choose. But just because I'm aware of it doesn't mean I have to *like* it when I watch another cock ravage your tiny, tight cunt," he snarls. Reaching me, he pins the covers to either side of my torso with his hands as he leans over me, warm breath bathing my skin as he bites out, "When I observe him spend his seed within your hot sex and hear you call out another's name in ecstasy."

My air comes out in little pants as I stare into his furious expression. "Why—why watch if you don't want to see?" I manage to squeak.

He growls, a long low threatening sound that reverberates down in his chest as he leans his face to within inches of mine. It's scary and incredibly arousing both, doing things deep inside my body. Following an instinct that isn't even a conscious thought, I tilt my head further, exposing my throat more.

"Because you called out to me and once here, I can't resist watching you cum. It's fucking spectacular. *Every. Single. Damn. Time.*" He licks a long slow line up my neck, stopping at my pulse beating like a frantic bird trapped under my skin.

"I didn't—I didn't mean to," I stutter as his teeth bite down, then release with a lick over the spot.

"I'm aware, but you are *my* writer. You know I will come to you when you call. Choose your words more wisely in the future, little one. I only have so much control. Watching another take what I consider mine as you shout out to me in the throes of your passion is just begging me to prove my claim in the rawest ways possible," he snarls.

He takes a few measured breaths that shiver over my skin before continuing, "I've been letting you get used to me, easing you and preparing you over these last weeks. You aren't yet ready for how thoroughly I'll brand your body as mine. Be careful, darling. I only have so much patience and control." Loki closes his eyes for several minutes, breathing deeply against my neck with his nose buried in my hair.

I'm conflicted. Fuck, but I want to touch him, pull him down and hug him. I crave his dominant, possessive, animalistic nature. I love the way I feel in response to it—desirable, wanton, and so very feminine—but I also need him to respect my boundaries. We haven't discussed any kind of commitment between us other than sensual exploration. He's given every indication that he finds it hot as hell to share me, despite his possessiveness. Damn it all. It's not like Loki is even capable of being monogamous himself when I write him to be with another of my characters.

And maybe I owe him an apology. It hadn't occurred to me that my choice of exclamation would be taken as calling for him. Knowing his nature and possessive inclinations, I would not have put him in that position on purpose.

At least, not consciously. His response is incredibly hot. God, I'm quivering from his words alone, so I'm not entirely sure if I'm lying to myself or not. Maybe I would have.

"I am sorry, Loki. I wasn't trying to wind you up intentionally," I tell him quietly, despite my internal confusion.

When his head lifts and his eyes open again, the rage is gone and a sensual warmth has replaced it. "At least the water washed his scent and seed from you so you don't stink of him. I'd much rather have you smell of me." Closing the distance between our faces, he kisses me in a surprisingly tender but thorough caress and the tension in my body eases.

He leans on an arm and one knee, tugging the covers off me.

"Loki, what—" He stops my words with a finger pressed to my lips.

"I know your little human form is wrung out and needs rest." His lips twitch up in reluctant approval. "I give James high marks for creative use of the hot tub jets. That was truly inspired on his part. I'm just going to hold you and sleep with you tonight. Is that okay with you?" He lifts his finger so I can answer.

"Yes, Loki. I'd like that." I smile as he removes his clothes and rolls in behind me, pulling the covers back over us.

After sliding an arm under my neck, he tucks my head into his shoulder even as his body curls around me. He shifts me until his leg is bent between my thighs with my hips tilted toward the bed so that I'm riding the firm muscle against my core. His hand is on the waistband of my panties for a second before a sudden, hard jerk rips them off me with a quick sting of pain, and then the fabric gives way to Loki's strength.

My lips twitch. "I thought you wanted me to sleep."

The rumble of his laugh vibrates against me. "Sure, but I needed that."

I hide my smile behind my hand. Despite the extra expense and illogical nature of it, the dominance of him tearing off my clothes creates a warm glow and deep satisfaction within my chest.

He shifts his leg against my core, putting pressure on my clit, and I jolt before he stops moving. "I do want you to sleep, but I still enjoy the wet heat of your pussy against my skin. If I get my cock against it, well... you won't be sleeping. This is my compromise," he purrs into my ear even as he nudges me in the back with the hard, hot evidence of his arousal.

I bite my lip, and my sex clenches—another wave of moisture flooding my folds—tantalized by his sleekly masculine body entwined with mine, desiring me. His contented rumble resonates against my torso as he notices.

"Mmm... so responsive to me, even as tired as you are. How you tempt me to ignore my better judgment."

His arm slides over my waist, and his hand slips under my t-shirt to cup my breast. It's such a possessive position with him wrapped around me, but it feels good. Safe. Wanted. Protected and cared for.

"Go to sleep, little writer. Rest and recover. I'll try to wait until morning to ravish this sexy little body."

Despite the erotic potential of his hold, I'm cocooned in his heat and scent. His breath wafts over my hair, and his heartbeat soothes me as I drift off.

CHAPTER ELEVEN

Nerves

Nerves flutter in my belly as I hit the button to send the current chapter of *Hidden* to my beta-readers. I'm proud of what I've written and am fairly confident that they will like the blend of humour and tension between my main characters, Shannon—a human scientist turned Elven immortal goddess, and Loki—Asgard's Black Prince. Yeah, it isn't my readers I'm worried about.

You know what I'm nervous about, don't you?

How could you not? You've seen how he reacts when he's not happy with me. I'm still waiting for the other shoe to drop from him sharing me with his brother, from him watching me with James. As much as he wants to see me, his little writer, well fucked and limp with multiple orgasms, Loki has been clear that it will trigger his ruthlessly possessive instincts. It's making me jumpy as the weeks progress, and he hasn't followed through with his erotic promise to claim me, to brand my body as his, to fuck me so thoroughly I'd never doubt his ownership.

And it *is* a promise, not a threat. Remembering his words in that low growled tone gets me hot whenever I think about it. My hand trembles as I tuck a lock of hair back behind my ear, then rub my slightly sweaty palms on my red flannel pyjama bottoms.

I'm sure he is going to act one of these days. He has this specific look, a particularly wicked smile that lets me know he's thinking about it. Every time he smiles at me like that, the slow, uneven smirk that curls up, then widens with his emerald eyes dark with sinful intention, my heart races, wondering if today is the day.

But so far, it hasn't been.

So you bet your ass I'm nervous after having the audacity to write Shannon taunting and teasing him. It's a bit like poking a panther. He has that wild unpredictability to him... he is the God of Chaos, after all.

But he was fine by the end of the chapter though, right? *Right?!*

I blow out a long, shaky breath and get up from my computer. Nothing for it but to wait to see. I walk to my kitchen and when I'm almost through the doorway, I rethink my destination.

Probably not a smart idea to find myself near the island counter right after taunting the trickster, especially since I'm the one that will end up paying the price. I laugh nervously, running my fingers through my long brown hair and shoving it back from my face. Not that I didn't enjoy the brothers bending me over the cold granite, because well, of course I did, but still.

It's just tempting fate to go in there right now, even if part of me yearns to experience that again.

Pressing a hand to my belly, it's doing flips and adding anything to it will probably make me more queasy. Perhaps I won't eat breakfast this morning.

Changing direction, I round the corner and head upstairs. As I climb the creaking wood treads of the renovated Victorian, I smell a hint of citrus and fresh-cut timber. Stopping, I turn, but I don't see him anywhere.

Maybe it's just my holiday decorations.

With Christmas only a few days away, I spent all day yesterday wrapping newly cut cedar and pine boughs from my yard into wreaths for the doors and the bottom post of the stairs, hanging lights, and finally putting up a fir tree in the family room. The holidays are lonely since my grandmother's passing and while a couple of friends have invited me over, I don't want to crash their family time. My house is festive, even if I'm having a harder time convincing myself to enjoy the spirit of celebration. I'll probably just make myself a nice meal and watch *Pride and Prejudice* like I did last year.

I lift a hand to brush my hair back from my eyes again, and my fingers tremble, the scent still surrounding me. Both provoking and tantalizing, it seems to wrap around my body in a physical caress. Hand gripping the dark oak stair rail, I take a few deep breaths, exhaling slowly to try to calm the butterflies desperately fluttering in a mad panic to escape my belly.

Damn it. It's not like he'd hurt me. Stop being such a ninny. I'm his writer. He needs me.

But my nerves are irrational. They don't listen to my attempts to use logic. The unsettled sensation follows me as I continue up the rest of the stairs and into my bedroom.

Why am I nervous? This is just ridiculous. I'm ridiculous. He'll probably just fuck me senseless. I roll my eyes and kick the thick wooden post of my bed.

I *love* what he does to me. It's amazing every single time.

There is absolutely no reason to be skittish. Gah, I'm being so... a memory washes over me—him thrusting, hard and deep, his lips on mine as he steals my soul and the very breath from my lungs. A heated shiver crawls up my abdomen as my core dampens with remembered pleasure and my skin prickles.

With rough tugs, I yank my arms out of my t-shirt and haul it over my head. Grinding my teeth as my nipples tighten in the cool air, I snag the waist of my pyjama bottoms and tug them down my legs.

In a flash of insight, I realize why my emotions are in turmoil, flip-flopping like the weather in spring.

I am constantly aroused lately... a hum in my body that won't go away. And I know why. Loki has been visiting at least twice a week—sometimes more, but never less—every week for the past two months. But I haven't seen him in the last two weeks.

Not. Even. Once.

Not since he woke me to pleasure me thoroughly after James' visit.

My body is letting me know, in demanding fashion, that it misses the regular dose of rapture. Every damn morning for seven days in a row, I've woken to the faint smell of oranges with earthy hints of leather and wood, drenched and aching from erotic fantasies that then haunt me the rest of the day. I manage to distract myself with writing, grocery shopping, holiday decorating or baking, but invariably, my mind returns to him.

And each time I remember how it feels to be with Loki, the things he's done in my dreams or my conscious hours, my body wakes and yearns for his touch.

Despite that, I've been completely unable to get myself off.

At all.

Not once.

No matter how many times I've attempted it over the week. God, have I tried. Over and over.

From my dresser, I take a clip and pin my waist-length hair up on top of my head as I let out a growl. I'm frustrated. Incredibly, teeth-grittingly frustrated.

That's the problem with really excellent sex. Once you've had it, nothing else will satisfy. It has me seriously contemplating gifting myself sex toys for Christmas. I've even bookmarked a few, made a list, and started reading reviews. But if I can't get myself off now, will I have better luck with toys? I've never had a hard time masturbating before.

It's kind of an essential skill, after all. The men I've dated frequently lack in their ability to bring me to orgasm before they climax, but I've always been able to finish myself off when the sex has fallen flat.

Not that sex has ever failed to be spectacular with Loki. He seems to view my initial orgasm as a warm-up, like they are potato chips and you can never just stop at one. No, he wants the entire bag, and he's going to feed them to me exactly the way he demands, each and every time. Until I'm limp with satiation.

God, I've never been with anyone like him before. In the past, it's always been an equal partnership in the bedroom. I've never felt the need to submit, to want to be dominated by such an overwhelming masculine presence.

Okay, that's not true.

An icy chill shivers down my spine as bend to snag my t-shirt and pyjama bottoms from the floor, then dump them into the wicker laundry hamper next to my oak dresser.

I know I'm lying to myself. Yeah, I've wanted it, but I've never allowed myself to act on it. I've never trusted someone enough to give up control, never been secure in the knowledge that they would ensure my pleasure and safety.

As I wrap my arms around myself, I swallow past the lump in my throat, remembering. The previous time I'd considered opening up about my desires still haunts me. Even though my boyfriend and I had been dating for three years, I'd hesitated, scared to tell him my true needs.

A wise decision, as it turned out.

Better if I hadn't dated the fucker at all.

Squeezing my eyes shut, I can't prevent the image of him from coming to mind—cock buried in another woman on our apartment table when I'd walked in, tears streaming down my face and trying to hold in sobs after the phone call that my grandmother had died of a sudden aneurysm. Like a blurry scene through a rain-soaked window, it still has the power to tighten my chest, pain a vice around my heart.

My fingers dig into my arms. Despite the two and a half years that have passed, I haven't been able to forget. Trust has been in short supply... until Loki.

But maybe Loki has decided he's had enough. A sinking sensation settles into my gut. Maybe that's why he hasn't visited in the last couple of weeks.

CHAPTER TWELVE

Frustration

After slowly walking to the bathroom, I turn on the shower and hold my hand in the flow as I wait for the water to get up to temperature. It's not just my skin that's chilled—ice freezes deep inside me as I consider how lonely the last two weeks have been. How facing another Christmas on my own has me not wanting to bother making the effort.

Still, better cold and alone than betrayed.

Steam begins to billow out of the tiled enclosure. I step under the heated spray, letting the warmth sink into my body. It chases away the chill of traumatic memory as my muscles gradually relax. I focus on my breathing, envisioning the image of my ex-boyfriend flowing out of my brain and washing down the drain with the water.

Into the sewer where he belongs.

And well, if Loki is done visiting me here in the real world, I'll never regret the time he spent with me.

With a flick of my thumb, I open my lemon vanilla body wash, inhaling the favourite scent... okay, second favourite since a certain orange, leather, and wood blend has replaced it. Still, I upend the bottle and squeeze some onto my exfoliating sponge and start scrubbing my arms. My hands slow as I recall Loki's hands caressing my body, his fingers featherlight in their teasing as my blood turns to molten honey. Arousal reignites and I shiver, nipples tightening while I tilt my flushed face into the water.

Loki makes me nervous.

He also makes me feel feminine, desirable, and free to be passionate. It's not a scared nervousness that has my pulse fluttering and butterflies stirring in my abdomen. No, not with him. Instead, it's nerves mixed with anticipation, because when he visits, he pushes my limits beyond the safe, ordinary, maybe slightly boring sex I've enjoyed in the past. I want that push, but I can't make myself ask for it. Not after—

Yet Loki knows. I might get in his head as his writer, but somehow, he's gotten into mine as well.

Soaping my breasts, they're heavy and aching, and my fingers massage and tug on the tips. God, but I wish these were his hands. His touch. The arousal that's plagued me all week flares to new heights, and I can't help wanting to be touched. It's become a craving in my flesh, an itch driving me crazy.

Fisting the sponge, I wash my stomach, my hips, and move down my legs to my feet. The water and soap slide sensuously over my skin. After rising from my bent position, I rinse the loofa and use my fingers to clean my inner thighs and core. Unable to resist, I brace my other arm against the shower wall, shuddering as my fingertips glide over the swollen, sensitive nub. Teasing myself, my fingertips circle a few times before stopping. I'm slippery and flushed, but I'm not willing to bring myself to the edge again when I can't seem to orgasm.

Sex toys. I definitely need to buy myself some damn sex toys. Surely with them, I can finally break this dry streak.

I snort. Dry. Fuck, I'm anything *but* dry.

My frustration has me slapping the water off and stepping out of the shower with a huff of annoyance. As I reach for a towel, the scent of citrus and the warmth of fresh-cut timber surrounds me, but there's no one in the bathroom. My Christmas tree is downstairs. I don't even have a pine wreath up here. Frowning, I bring the woven cloth to my nose, but it just smells of the faint fresh rain scent I use for my laundry soap and fabric softener.

Impatiently, I drag the material over my body. Its texture is rough as I scrub the water off with too much force, trying to tamp down the arousal in my touch-hungry skin.

"I am clearly losing my damn mind. Stupid sexual frustration!" I shout into the empty space.

With the wet towel in my hands, I stomp naked back to my bedroom and swipe up the hamper. Then I head to the laundry room situated off the main bathroom and between the two other bedrooms. They're for guests now since I finally moved out of my childhood room and into the main bedroom. Not that I have guests often, except for the occasional sleepover when my friends drink too much during my rare parties.

I open the front-loading washer with a harsh tug and stuff clothes in, grumbling to myself. I can't be bothered to sort the colours from the whites, but at this point, who cares if my towels turn a bit pink? Not me, that's for damn sure. Slamming the door shut, I stretch up to reach for the soap. Ugh. One of these days I'm going to hire a handyman to put in a shelf lower than the current six-and-a-half foot one. I mean, I know I don't want to bash my head on the shelf when I use the laundry tub, but standing on my tiptoes every time to stretch for the soap or dryer sheets has me growling.

Goddamn it, the metal washer is frigid against my bare skin as I withdraw a soap pod, then fumble the slippery thing to watch it hit my breast, bounce onto the washer, then roll off the side between the washer and the laundry sink, and splat on the tile.

"Oh for fuck's sake!" I snarl, bending to reach under the open plastic legs of the tub. I snatch up the little blue pod, stand and shove it in the soap dispenser, stabbing buttons with my fingertips. A shushing, trickling sound comes from the machine as it starts its cycle.

"That was just fucking ridiculous," I mutter as I stomp to my bedroom and stare at my oak dresser, hands on my hips. With no plans to go out, I yank open a wooden drawer that squeals in protest and select black panties and a bra. Shutting the drawer with a bang, I jerk open another and remove dark blue leggings. After slamming that drawer closed with my hip, I drag the clothes on. From my walk-in closet, I snatch a royal blue scoop-neck, hip-length sweater off a hanger and tug it roughly over my head. After pulling the clip from my hair to let the heavy brown mass fall down my back and tossing the clip onto my dresser, I'm done getting ready.

My earlier nervousness has been completely overtaken by simmering frustration. Damn it, I could use a walk to expend some of this energy, but the weather is shitty outside. Sleet started hitting the roof a few minutes ago and just a glance out my balcony patio door has me shivering. I want nothing more than to curl up in front of the fire and distract myself with a story, something other than my own.

With heavy steps, I thump down the creaking stairs, turn the corner and enter my family room. After turning on the gas fireplace—thank god that was one of the renovations we'd done years ago to get rid of the wood-burning stove—I flop onto a worn but comfortable grey fabric couch and snag my tablet off the sturdy pine-topped coffee table. Surely I can find something to distract myself. But flipping through my library, I groan. Opal Reyne, Ruby Dixon, Nalini Singh, Christine Feehan—All the authors' stories I have lined up to read next have smoking hot males and sex in them.

Disgusted, I toss my tablet onto the cushion, close my eyes, tug my hair with my hands, and let out a brief scream.

"What's the matter, little writer? You seem a bit... frustrated."

CHAPTER THIRTEEN

Rules

My eyes flash open to see Loki sitting on the couch across from me. The tightness in my chest loosens, and I don't want to think too much about why. A small part of my mind wonders how he suddenly appears in my reality—a question I haven't found any real answer to over these last weeks since he first arrived—yet the rest of me is consumed by the heat swamping me as I devour the sight of him.

More casually dressed without his silver Asgardian armour, he is the epitome of tall, dark, and handsome in black leather pants and an ebony tunic that hugs his wide shoulders, muscular torso, and thighs. Not bulky, he has an athlete's build full of lean muscle and the monochromatic style contrasts beautifully with his pale skin and midnight hair. But it's the edge of danger, that lethal aura he gives off that is the true seduction. With a single glance, he has my sex clenching and a wave of gooseflesh chasing the erotic shiver teasing my flesh.

Reclined with one arm thrown over the couch back and his ankle resting on his knee in a characteristic male spread, his emerald eyes are alight with sin and amusement, a small knowing smirk on his face.

I cross my arms to hide my body's instant reaction, even as I finally register his words. "Why do you think I might be frustrated?" Did he see me throw the tablet? Is it my expression? The scream?

His smile widens, and he gestures toward me with a negligent hand. "You mean other than the adorable little temper tantrum, flushed cheeks, the way you are squeezing your thighs together restlessly, and attempting to hide those lusciously peaked nipples from me?"

I hadn't realized I was fidgeting and attempt to stop. Yet, it's hard to resist. My skin prickles with awareness, like there is an electric charge between us, even with him on the far side of the room. It's ratcheted up the tension in my body, feeding my frustration. He hasn't touched me, but I'm drenched by his presence, the caress of his sinful deep voice over my senses. A second heartbeat throbs in my sex.

"Okay, maybe I am," I admit, unable to keep the snarkiness out of my tone.

One eyebrow raised and eyes darkening, his fingers drum his thigh. His tone conveys his arrogance as he asks, "Are you giving me attitude?"

I shrug a shoulder. "So what if I am?" Even as the words leave my lips, I know I shouldn't have.

I don't see him move. One minute he is seated, and in the next heartbeat, he's leaning over me, hand wrapped around my throat, pinning me to the back of the couch as a gasp escapes me. His eyes glitter with lustful intent, mouth twisted into a satisfied smile.

My pulse flutters in my veins. Anticipation and nerves heat my abdomen in a twisting, churning desire as my breath shortens to pants.

"I was so hoping you'd give me an excuse, little writer," he growls in a low erotic purr that vibrates deep in my core.

He presses a firm kiss to my lips, and a falling sensation has me yelping and jolting to grab him before I find myself flat on my back, hands on his shoulders, legs around his waist with him pushing me down, still pinning me with a hand at my throat.

As our mouths part, my head spins with confusion. We're in my bedroom, on my four-poster king-sized bed, with the wooden ceiling fan visible behind Loki's shoulder.

"How?"

His smile widens, and he laughs. The darkly sinful sound ripples down my spine in an almost physical caress. Lowering his hips to mine, he grinds his straining erection against my soaked core, drawing a needy whimper from my throat.

"You didn't realize that I still have all my powers and abilities here? Oh, dear. My poor, little, naïve writer."

Each word mocks me with his delight, his ruthless intent, and my eyes widen, unable to stop squirming beneath him.

He shakes his head and gives me a positively evil smile. "I'm not just your character, I'm a *god*. Who do you think has been playing with you all week? I can't begin to tell you how much I've enjoyed bringing you to a fever pitch each night, leaving you so achingly wet and pleading for me, and then observing you try to satisfy yourself when I allow you to wake. Norns, I do love watching you in the shower, your body all slippery and soaked, water caressing every curve of this sexy, made-for-sinning form."

My hand is in motion before I can think better of it, and the loud crack across his cheek is shocking in the quiet of my bedroom. I gasp, shaking my stinging palm while I wait for him to retaliate.

He leans down to my ear, nuzzling his face against mine, then nipping my earlobe sharply with his teeth as his deep growl shivers down my body. His fingers continue squeezing my neck before easing up slightly. "Clearly, I've been neglecting your lessons in discipline. Such a feisty little writer when I don't let you cum for a few days. You've earned yourself a lesson in delayed gratification."

My heart leaps, and I can't help but blurt out, "But isn't that what you've been doing this week?" in a panicked squeak.

Wickedly dark amusement infuses his growled reply, "That was just a taste. An appetizer to whet your appetite. Time now for the *real* instruction to begin. Fair warning. I'm not going to stop you, so if you cum before I allow it, you'll get no orgasms for the next month."

"*What?*" I exclaim, shocked.

"Keep giving me attitude, darling, and I can make it two very slow, cold, lonely winter months. With a simple hypnotic suggestion, my powers will ensure you can't give yourself any for however long I wish. Do you understand?"

It takes me a minute to close my mouth. Fuck, he's totally evil. Not a god, he's definitely the devil. A seductive, evil, fucking hot devil.

"Yes, Loki," I finally grumble, fists clenched in his tunic.

Damn it, I want to smack him again. While I'd like to dismiss it as an empty threat, I'm not willing to chance it. I can't believe I didn't know he could use his powers here, but he gives me no time to dwell on this new revelation.

"I'm sorry. I don't think I heard you?" His warning rumble and squeezing fingers around my neck have me biting back my petulance.

CHAPTER FOURTEEN
Playing A Symphony

Holy hell. He is really *not* playing around. The nervous butterflies are back in a mad fluttering dance within my insides. What is he going to do to me? Will I be able to take it? What if it's too much? Two months is a freaking long damn time after discovering how satisfying sex can be with him.

I gaze up into his dark eyes and the small smirk on his lips. There is no give in his expression, in the fingers around my throat, or the rigid cock pressing against my core.

"Yes, Loki," I say meekly as the reality of my predicament sinks in.

After releasing my neck and shifting his weight off me, he bends my legs, pushing my knees up to my shoulders, keeping them spread apart. With a flash of swirling black seidhr rippling over me, my clothes are gone.

Fuck, I can't believe I didn't know he can use his magic and abilities in my reality. It's a complete game-changer, and I'd be lying to myself if I don't acknowledge this arouses me further.

Taking my arms, he has me hold my knees. "Keep them there, no matter what. If you don't, I'll tie them in place, and I'll bloody well enjoy the sight of my ropes around you. Tell me you understand," he demands, looking into my eyes.

In this position, I'm completely exposed to him, utterly vulnerable. Not just physically, but emotionally, too. He's cowed me entirely.

But something about that, about submitting to his will, lets me relax. Like knowing I don't have to be in charge, I don't have to make any decisions... it flips a switch within me and gives me permission to sink into the sensations. Despite past experience with others, at this moment, I trust him entirely. I know he'll ensure my safety and enjoyment. While he likes to push me, to stretch my boundaries, he constantly checks I'm enjoying our play and I'm not in actual pain or distress.

"Yes, Loki," I answer obediently.

With two fingers, he traces along my inner thighs and over my outer lips with a featherlight touch. I suck in a breath and my skin trembles.

"So very beautiful. It is intoxicating to see you soft, wet, and succulent, flushed this gorgeous rose. I think it's my favourite colour."

His smile turns predatory as he dips those long digits into my drenched core, stroking them in and out. I can't help but moan. God, he's got such clever fingers. There's no uncomfortable stabbing or scraping of fingernails or rough calluses on delicate flesh with him. Instead, he always seems to know the most tantalizing spots to curl those fingertips over to create delicious heat zinging up nerve endings as my sex squeezes around him.

Drawing his fingers out, covered in my slippery arousal, he drags them over to my ass and circles over the puckered rosette. Sensitive, I gasp in reaction to the darkly erotic caress. It makes me rock slightly as he repeats his actions, coating my back entrance. I want to squirm, but I can't let go of my legs. I know if I do, he'll follow through with his threat to tie me in place, and I don't want to fail. Why the idea of failure bothers me so much, I'm not sure, but I dig my fingertips deeper into my flesh.

Locking eyes with me, he circles and circles in a seductive dance before pressing in with a single finger.

I suck in a sharp breath at the tantalizing sensation of just his fingertip dipping in and out. It's indescribably dirty, yet intoxicating. The tingling warmth radiating into my pelvis and up my spine has me shivering.

"You enjoy that, don't you? You like my finger fucking your tight little ass?" he asks in a seductive purr.

I can't look away from the knowing gleam in Loki's seductive eyes. God, how does he know? It's as if he sees right into my soul... every dark, forbidden corner. He brings my desires to light, even when I'm unwilling to acknowledge them.

"Answer me," he demands.

"Yes," I moan, surrendering.

The warm, tingling sensation increases and spreads. It would be so easy to allow myself to sink into it and permit the feeling to overwhelm my senses, let the climax flow over me. But I can't. God, I want to though. Two months. I need to resist it. Fuck.

"Did you know, my kinky little writer," he says in a sinful purr as his fingertip continues its seductive probing, "That there are five major nerves pathways in your exquisitely sexy body I can exploit in different ways to have you cumming whenever I want?"

I'm quivering around his finger, trying to hold back the orgasm shimmering along those nerves as he strokes in and out. Fuck, it's been too long, too many hours, so close, so needy.

"Loki! I need to cum." Please, God. *Please.*

"No." Despite his flat denial, I'm about to lose control when he suddenly stops moving.

I groan, gritting my teeth and shaking with the craving to give in. It's a desperate struggle not to.

With a small smile on his face, he waits.

And waits.

My heartbeat slows, and the sensation fades. He winks, and once again, he moves, this time sinking his finger in all the way to his knuckles. I suck in a breath, moaning as he reverses his stroke to send a spike of heat flaring up my spine. It's both heaven and hell.

"This tiny ass that is gripping my finger so tight? It's connected to a couple of those pathways. Can you feel it?" he purrs.

"Yes, god yes." The tingling spreads along my sparking nerve endings, creating a fever in my flesh. My skin prickles with it.

His eyes are dark pools as he watches his finger, delving in and out. "I'm going to strum all five nerves and create a symphony of your beautiful moans before you are allowed to cum. You, my deliciously responsive little writer, are a delight to play with."

My head drops back to the bed, panting and looking at the ceiling. "Oh my god." Desperately, I'm trying to not squirm or rock myself against his finger. It would take so very little to send me over the edge. Two months. Fuck.

"Yes. Yes, I am. And you would do well to not forget it," he growls.

Leaning his head down to my pussy, his tongue teasingly traces the edges of both outer lips before circling my opening to lightly dip inside. "Mmm... sweet and salty, with a hint of musky earthiness, almost like wood smoke."

My whine erupts in a half-whimper, half-laugh. "You make me sound like a whiskey vintage."

He taps my clit, and I can't control the gasp and involuntary jerk that rocks me in place with the jolt that single touch sent through my abdomen.

"So much better than whiskey," he purrs.

I lose my train of thought as his stiff tongue flicks hard and fast, lightning blasting through my core to join the slower-rising fever from the continued erotic penetration of my ass. Like an express elevator, I'm shooting for the top floor, about to burst right out of the roof.

"Loki, please!" I beg, squirming in my attempt to control the rising sensual tide. Failing, my fingernails desperately dig into my thighs. Fuck. Something. Anything to distract myself from the heat swamping me.

"Don't you dare cum," he warns even as the wave is rising, rising, rising, and then—

Nothing.

He stops completely, lifting his head to meet my gaze.

CHAPTER FIFTEEN
Start Counting

U nable to look away, my pulse throbs like a second heartbeat in my core. Each beat pounds a tempo demanding satisfaction.

I clench my jaw against the scream I want to let loose.

He waits, his smile slowly widening.

The trembling within my muscles eases, and I manage to stop my desperate squirming, finally drawing in a breath that doesn't shake or heave, but it's by no means steady.

Lowering his head, his tongue avoids my clit to lick and suck on nearby flesh. And in between, he purrs, "We're halfway there. Two more nerves to join in the symphony we're creating."

I try to answer through panted breaths, and it comes out as a garbled whine. Fuck, I want to swear at him, but I bite back the words. He'll make me pay if I do, and oh god, I don't think I can take more.

His eyes gleam as if he knows the curses I'm biting back. "Very eloquent, but it just happens to be my favourite song. Let's see how my Melody changes when we add additional instruments, shall we?" he growls against my clit. Flattening his tongue, he lathes over it as two long fingers plunge inside my slippery core, even as his other digit continues its relentless stroking in and out of my ass.

"Loki!" I whimper, squirming as he alternates between sucking and licking with his mouth, his fingers keeping their rhythm. Curling the ones in my pussy, he strums over my G-spot.

I can't stay still. It's too much. Even with the position I'm in. Desperately, I cling to my knees as my hips writhe violently, rocking and bucking in place.

It's blazing hotter, the flames building and tingling out from my core in a relentless, rushing forest fire up my abdomen, down my thighs, spreading and spreading. Like the sudden flashover of an influx of oxygen to a burning house, it starts to expand to the rest of my body.

He stops.

Removes his hand from my straining body.

Freezes his tongue, lifting it away.

"*No!* Oh my god! *Please!*" I scream, pleading with him as I pant and writhe.

His fierce glare locks onto me, trapping my gaze. "What? You don't think it's *fair*, considering you've been teasing and taunting me? Don't deny it, you know you have. First with the last chapter, then I saw what you wrote and made real in the story with today's upload," he snarls.

"It will be worth it with what's coming up," I grit out as my eyes narrow. Part of me wants to bite or scratch him. My nails dig into my legs. Violence at being denied is a hot ember, glowing and burning within my chest.

"Hmm... perhaps, but you agreed to my terms." He holds my gaze for another minute, his own eyes still savage. His expression is unyielding at first, but then slowly changes as his scorching eyes rove over my body before returning to my face.

"Fuck!" I curse, shaking and sweaty with need, a fine layer of moisture coating my flushed skin.

"Does it make you feel better to know the frustration isn't one-sided?" His voice loses the angry snarl, sliding back to a sultry growl. "When I haven't been tortured with Shannon's touch and scent in the other world, it's been your sexy little body driving me insane in this one."

Lifting me with effortless strength, he flips me onto my stomach, pulling my ass up, and pushing my head down to the bed. Fitting his hips to mine, he grinds his leather-covered erection against my soaked core.

I whimper before scowling back at him. "You probably jerked off tons of times."

Continuing to grind, his voice lowers to a seductive caress of my senses that has me writhing, panting, and lifting my ass to meet him like a cat in heat. "Ah, but I didn't. *Not. Even. Once.* After all, I wasn't allowing you to cum without me and knew you weren't letting me have Shannon. And I've absolutely *ached* to sink my cock in your scorchingly tight, wet little cunt. I'm impressed you lasted a full week before giving in to your temper."

"Loki, please," I cry, tears of frustration prickling behind my eyes as I try to shove at his clothes to remove them. "Please. I can't take any more teasing!"

"Almost there, my beautiful Melody," he purrs. His shirt and pants disappear. Hot, blunt flesh poises at my entrance. Loki grips my hair, yanking my head back. His other hand dives under my torso to cup my breast, rolling a taut peak between the knuckles of two fingers. "There is one last nerve we haven't added to our song yet. It's triggered when I do this." He pinches my nipple with a ruthless twist. At the same time, his hips drive forward, burying his thick cock inside me to the hilt in a single powerful thrust.

A scream tears out of my throat at the intense combination, electricity exploding through my body, blinding my vision for a few seconds and I shake, my muscles quivering.

Loki begins to move in short rocking thrusts. He grunts with each flex of his hips. "Damn. Your little cunt is clamped so fucking tight, I don't want to hurt you."

"No, it's good. So good," I gasp. He's hitting that spot deep inside that has my eyes crossing and shudders flaring up my spine. "Keep doing that," I moan as I rock my hips to meet his short movements.

"Getting bossy, are we?" he asks, tugging my hair in warning.

"Yes... oh *god!* Please let me cum, Loki. *Please*," I whine as the trembling in my muscles increases.

He withdraws almost all the way out, the wide head poised at my entrance, before sliding his cock in again, starting a longer, deeper rhythm of pulling out to the edge, only to plunge to the hilt each time.

Whimpering at the friction of his thick cock riding my inner walls, I shake. The fiery warmth that had been banked down to embers each time he'd delayed my orgasm flares into a raging inferno, radiating throughout my pelvis, down my thighs, up my abdomen, and over my sweat-slick skin with each pounding stroke.

He increases his speed, plunging hard and fast. Each jolting impact brings me closer than the last.

"Loki, please." God, I'm going to lose my mind if he stops me this time.

I can't take it.

Fuck, I can't take it.

I can't hold back.

"Oh my god, *please!*"

"Cum for me," he demands as his hips slam into my pelvis. My back arches, nerves scorching as the orgasm rips up my spine and out the top of my head in a rush like a volcanic eruption. As I shatter into a million pieces, my body bucking with intense contractions, he groans deeply into my neck, his cock flooding his release inside me.

We pant for a minute until he tugs my hair to meet his gaze, and with a wink, says, "Now let's see how many times I can make you cum in the next twenty-four hours. That's one."

Don't Taunt The Trickster

Episode Three Description

When my fictional character invaded my reality, this writer resorts to underhanded tricks of her own to deal with Loki.

***

Asgard's Black Prince warned me. From the beginning, he's said he wants my attention and he's not a fan of sharing. Yet, despite all the possessive looks and words, he's yet to follow through. Maybe he's all hot air, but that's not how I've written the character. Perhaps Loki needs a little more inspiration to finally act. He's certainly got me curious to see what else he might have in store for me. Sometimes to get what you want, you have to play dirty.

CHAPTER SIXTEEN

Gods Gotta Eat, Too

The weather is perfect for my barbeque, with enough breeze blowing in off the lake to keep the mosquitoes away and a brilliant blue sky with not a cloud in sight. So rare in March, but I'm not complaining. I lift my bare legs to rest them on the black wicker ottoman with its dark red pillow, tucking my short sundress under my thighs so the wind won't blow the hem up to my waist. I don't need to be flashing my panties at my friends.

"How's the writing going?" asks Nicole as she sips a glass of my special sangria recipe.

It's my typical party drink when I have company over. The four-litre pitcher almost overflowed when I'd blended the red wine, cherry brandy, cranberry-raspberry juice, and fresh fruit. Since I pre-soak the berries and cherries in brandy before adding them, my friends know from experience to enjoy them in moderation over the whole afternoon or they'll be sleeping in my guest bedrooms and on my couches.

Although, shit. I gaze down at my glass, full of berries. What will I do if Loki shows up and I have people staying the night? Maybe I don't want to encourage my company to crash here. Should I stop making my sangria so strong? Damn it. A fictional character shouldn't disrupt my life so thoroughly. How did everything get this complicated?

Sipping my drink, I attempt to ignore my swirling thoughts to focus on friends I haven't seen for weeks. "It's going well, I think. I know what the overall plot is for my fantasy romance trilogy, and I've got the details of the conspiracy thriller worked out," I tell her, without giving away any specifics that would spoil it for them. Not that they've read any of my chapters yet. Instead, I'm using beta-readers through an online website.

"My brother says his characters talk to him. Does it ever seem like that for you?" asks Claire, sitting on the other wicker couch across from Nicole and me.

Oh god! I choke on my drink, barely keeping my exclamation to myself. After a few coughs, I manage to wheeze, "Yes, mine are quite... interactive." Able to breathe again, I lift my drink to hide my nervous smile at that epically massive understatement. Not only can't I say what really has been happening over the last five months, but I have no way to explain it. My friends would think I'm completely nuts. And maybe I am. Still, I'd have better luck convincing them I'm haunted by ghosts than that my fictional characters aren't so fictional and jump realities from their universe to mine to become flesh and blood here on a regular basis.

Claire eyes me with a slight frown creasing her brow, and I hurry to add, "I certainly don't suffer from writer's block with their inspiration to keep me going."

"Yeah, I've been meaning to check out your stories," says Nicole, fishing a blueberry out of her glass and popping it into her mouth. "One of your characters is my favourite from those superhero movies—Thor, right?"

"Sexy Thor," adds Clarie with an exaggerated wink to me, then laughing at Nicole fanning herself with her hands.

"It is Thor, yes. But not the movie or comic Thor. I based mine on a blend of mythology, including Norse, Egyptian, West Coast First Nations, and others. He has a different backstory, family, and his abilities differ somewhat as well. And while his mortal persona resembles that actor in some physical ways, my Asgardian god is a redhead. Okay, to be fair, he's still totally built with a ripped warrior's physique, as both Odin and Thor are part Jotun. I've seen how much you drool over those muscles," I tease Nicole. "Let me know what you think when I publish the stories."

"Oh, I will! I can't wait to buy your books." She grins, putting her hand on her forehead and leaning against Claire as if she's about to swoon like one of those heroines in a bodice-ripper novel.

The three of us burst out laughing, and Claire drops a sangria-soaked ice cube down Nicole's blouse.

"Melody, do you have any more of this layered Mexican dip? Shane finished it off and we're starving," shouts John from the barbeque and outdoor counter where I set out the food and drinks, trying to be heard over Nicole's shrieks and curses.

"Hey, it's not my fault you wanted to race the kayaks! You just couldn't keep up with our awesomeness." Shane laughs as he gestures to himself and Samantha, sitting on bar stools at the counter. She rolls her eyes and chuckles.

"Sure, I'll bring more out," I say as I rise from the couch. A bit of a head rush hits me. Whoa. I better slow down on the sangria fruit myself, or I'll be the one crashing early. On slightly unsteady legs, I walk over, grab the empty dip bowl, and turn to enter the house.

"Do you want any help?" asks John, taking a step to follow me. "I can chop or mix."

A chef at a local restaurant, he always offers to assist, but since we're having the party to cheer him up after he and his boyfriend broke up, I'm trying to keep him surrounded by our friends. "Nah! I've got it. If you'd go ahead and put the burgers and dogs on the grill and take care of cooking them, that'd be great. They're in the cooler by your feet." As I wave him off with a smile, Samantha, his sister, gives me a discrete thumbs up.

After closing the patio door behind me, I leave the bowl by the cutting board on the island, then head to the fridge and start pulling out ingredients to make more layered dip, a cheese dip, and some fresh-cut veggies to go with it. Bent over, I'm searching in my pull-out can drawer for refried beans when two large hands grab my butt and knead it with an aggressive squeeze.

I gasp, heart leaping as I start to jerk upright and a hand presses down on my back.

"I swear, Melody, this sweetly curved ass of yours tempts me to keep you in this position and fuck you senseless." The voice is a familiar deep rumble.

My sex clenches even as I spy Thor behind me and he releases me. "What are you doing here?" I ask as shove the drawer closed, lean against it, and press my thighs together. He doesn't visit often, but every single time is memorable.

His darkening sapphire eyes make a slow, heated perusal that feels like a physical stroke of my bare feet, bare legs, short blue sundress with its flared mid-thigh skirt, fitted waist and bodice, lingering at my chest in a way that has my nipples tightening to aching peaks, before continuing up to meet my eyes. The desire in his gaze is unmistakable, as is the conspicuously large rigid length straining the buttons of his brown leather pants.

Once I notice, it's impossible to tear my eyes away from that mouth-watering sight. The memory of him driving thick and deep, stretching me to pleasurable pain, and rubbing every inch inside me has moisture flooding, readying me, and my pulse thunders in anticipation. I try to look away, but I'm caught tracing the strained white fabric over his powerful chest, shoulders, and bare muscular arms with tawny hair over golden skin. Lean hips and those strong, strong thighs. God, I want to rip away his tucked-in shirt to find those rock-hard abs. My fingertips itch to explore those steely ridges. Okay, so I'm eye-fucking him as much as he is me. It's true. C'mon. He's goddamn gorgeous. Wouldn't you?

"You were talking about me," he says with a sensual half-smile curving those very kissable lips.

His words jolt me out of my sensual haze, and I blink, taking a minute to catch up with their meaning.

Ah. Right. I should have anticipated that. Somehow my characters always seem to hear me when I say their name out loud. I snort to myself as a flash of emerald eyes surrounded by midnight hair appears in my mind's eye. Or even just what they consider their name.

"Yes, I suppose we were, but I have other humans over. I can't explain your presence here. They'd freak at the idea of gods and alien races from other planets and realities. Even if they don't, you'll soak every panty in the place..." My mind drifts to John. "And probably harden at least one cock, too. It'd be havoc. You're too damn gorgeous to unleash on my friends, Thor."

Thor's smile grows positively wicked, and there's a corresponding clenching in my sex as my pulse starts to thunder. "Don't worry about the mortals. They can't see me if I don't want them to."

Chapter Seventeen

Don't Say It

I blink and shake my head, trying to think through the cloud of lust surrounding me. How the hell does that work? If Thor is carrying me, would I appear to be levitating? Maybe I'm wrong. Maybe I can convince my friends that my house is haunted?

"What are you making?" he asks, gesturing at the ingredients on the black granite counter.

"A couple of dips and some cut veggies to go with them to take back outside." Distracted, I flick my fingers toward the windows to the backyard where my friends sit, visiting, drinking, and laughing.

"Don't stop on my account. I'm curious to watch you prepare a meal," he nods at the food even as his eyes spark, lightning flaring in their blue depths. His lips curl at the edges and I can't help but think he's up to some kind of mischief.

Huh. And here I thought his brother had the monopoly on that. I hold his gaze for a few moments and his expression doesn't change. Yeah, he's got some trouble in mind. Damn it, I just know I'm going to both love it and regret it. Here's hoping my friends don't come into the house anytime soon. With a few more suspicious glances towards him, I snag the can of refried black beans from the can drawer, open it, and empty the contents to layer on the bottom of the dip bowl. After cutting open the avocados, I scoop the flesh into a smaller bowl, adding lime juice, garlic, hot chilli, and salt.

Thor watches and it's impossible to not feel the heat of his eyes roving over me. When he moves behind me, his breath is a warm breeze tickling over the skin of my neck and shoulder. He smells like fresh rain and ozone, with a hint of pine forests in the summer heat. God, it's distracting. He's not touching me, but he's near enough that his body's presence is an electrical tingle against my skin. It makes me want to close the slight distance between us, to rub my face against his cheek and the rough red scruff as he peers over me. Or grind my ass back against his solid, thick body.

Fuck.

Why did I invite my friends over again?

His hands glide up the backs of my bare thighs sending sparks at his touch, and he leans into me, his voice a seductive rumble. "I enjoy watching you prepare food. I'm *hungry*." As his hands reach my butt, I realize he's been raising my skirt at the same time. That sensuous full mouth of his starts nibbling on my neck, and while one hand continues around my torso and up to my breast, the other strokes over my wet panties.

A shiver rakes my body, breath catching as my hands freeze with the masher mid-stroke.

"No... I want you to continue to prepare this meal while I play with you." Moisture trickles at his words. He slides his thick fingers under the edge of my panties, growling in approval.

Biting my lip, I close my eyes.

"You are so wet," he groans. "It's fucking hot. Continue, Melody, or I'll stop."

With shaking hands, I whimper and push the masher down.

His fingers trace along my seam, parting me with a broad finger and following it until he flicks a nail over my clit.

"Oh fuck," I gasp, my hips bucking at the electrifying touch.

His other hand kneads my breast, and I squirm, wanting his fingers on my aching nipples. Fingers clenched, I continue mashing the avocado mixture, turning it into guacamole despite my ragged breathing and heart thumping in my chest.

Toying with caresses through my curls and along the seam of my thighs, circling my clit, and then teasing the edges of my sex and back along the crease of my ass, Thor makes it insanely difficult for me to focus on what I'm doing. Sensation ripples like heat waves over me. Just as I think he's moving his hand away from where I most want it, he plunges two fingers inside, and I cry out as the pleasure flashes through my body like lightning, my knees weakening. My head falls back against his broad chest as I ride his thick digits.

But when I stop mashing, unable to coordinate my movements while chasing the ecstasy coiling in my abdomen, he stops moving and pins my hips between his body and the island so I'm unable to ride him. As soon as I return to making the food, he thrusts with his fingers again. His other hand alternates between my breasts, tugging on each nipple through the lace and fabric. My hands shake, and I'm chewing my lip to try to muffle my moans. God, I'm losing my fucking mind.

Over and over, this pattern repeats.

Every time I get too overwhelmed by the pleasure lighting up my veins and forget the next step to preparing the layer dip, then the cheese dip, and finally, cutting up the fresh vegetables, he stops and won't resume until I restart whatever step I'm doing.

By the time both dips are prepared and the veggies chopped, I'm panting, like I've run wind sprints. A fine layer of sweat shimmers over my skin and my thighs are soaked in my own arousal. I'm trembling with the force of his intoxicating storm. And holy god, I have no fucking idea how I'm still standing. Gratefully, I put down the twelve-inch chef's knife that forced me to concentrate while chopping even as my eyes crossed with sparks flaring within me.

A pleased rumble vibrates my back, and he presses against me, a rigid bar against my ass. "Now that I don't have to be concerned for the safety of your fingers, I can sink my aching cock into this drenched pussy." Thor tugs my panties down and replaces his fingers with that massive, steely length. Rubbing it over my soaked folds, he coats himself in slick fluids, then dips in and out of my entrance in a sinful tease.

"Thor, please. Oh god, please," I beg, shoving back against him as I brace myself on the counter.

His first rough thrust buries his cock to the hilt and has me keening while he groans. My core convulses around his invasive size, both pain and pleasure in the stretch—a confusing mix of erotic sensations.

"Fuck, you are so goddamn big, Thor!" I'm shaking like a leaf in a thunderstorm, lightning flaring across heightened nerve endings. Barely able to stand, I don't need to... he's holding my ass in place as I lean over the island.

"You know you can take it. The way your wet, needy pussy is squeezing and milking me, it wants me to pound it," he grits out as he holds back from moving.

He's right. I do want that. God, do I want it. Every fucking inch of him, as hard, deep, and fast as possible. He begins thrusting slowly. My fingers spasm on the cold granite, seeking purchase on the smooth stone while I tilt my ass like a cat in heat.

"Oh my god! Please, please god... fuck me harder, Thor," I plead, mewling, long and low.

"No. I'm taking my time to savour you this time," he groans against my ear as he licks and nibbles my neck. His slow pace is maddening as he builds the coiling tension with long, sure strokes. It has me squirming and whimpering.

Suddenly, he's pulling out.

"No! Goddamn it! Don't stop!"

His laugh is full of sensual amusement. "Patience, little one. I'll give you what you need." His fingers caress my skin, unzipping my dress to slide it off my shoulders. With a kiss along my spine, my bra follows.

In a fast unexpected move, he spins me to lift me onto the island on my back beside the food. Stepping between my legs, he slowly sinks his cock back in, drawing a long moan out of me as he continues his long, slow strokes in and out.

"Oh god, that is so, so good," I whimper, my head tossing back and forth.

Dipping his fingers into the layered dip, he scoops a handful out to smear over my breasts, then lowers his tongue to lap it up in long sweeps that match the strokes of his cock.

"Thor! Oh my god! Oh shit!" I cry out, writhing at the friction of his cock, the contrast of the cold dip and hot tongue sliding over my flesh.

"I want to eat all my food off your sexy little body," he rumbles as he scoops more dip over my skin. "I don't know how it tastes on its own, but it is fucking fantastic this way." He spends extra time sucking every drop from my nipples, and I know he can feel how it makes my core tighten around him—rumbles vibrating his throat every time I clench.

After a third round of eating the layered dip off my body, he starts to thrust faster.

"Yes, faster, please!"

"I want you to cum for me. I'm going to fill you up, then coat you in this other dip and eat it all from your creamy body."

"Oh my fucking god," I moan as the erotic imagery blends with the hard pounding thrusts to drive my arousal higher in sparking bursts.

"Now... now I want you to cum for me," he demands. The fine trembling in his limbs tells me how close he is himself.

"Oh my—" A pair of intense green eyes flash in my mind, and I bite the word off at the last second. Did I already say it? I did. A few times. But I shouldn't. He warned me, warned me there would be consequences to calling on him when another was fucking me. He's too possessive, too dominant to watch me be with another without staking his own claim.

But I want to. Make him watch. So bad. It is so fucking hot when he gets growly. And he's been teasing me with consequences for months. Nothing has happened. Maybe nothing well. Fuck, I want to.

No. Don't.

Behave. Don't say it. Don't think about him.

Say something else. Anything. Anything else.

"Oh, Thor!" Yes. Say that.

My mind swirls with conflicted desires as my orgasm peaks, and my core tightens in waves. Thor growls and pulses deep inside me, his hips pinned to mine as his powerful body jerks. Looking down at me, meeting my gaze, those dark blue eyes are still intense with passion, with lightning flaring and sparking in the depths.

He's clearly not done with me yet.

After pulling out, he takes the bowl of cheese dip and pours it over my abdomen. It's warm, but not hot, as his fingers draw it down between my thighs.

"Now, that is a feast," he says, a pleased smile on his face as he lowers his mouth.

I gasp, clinging to his tousled red locks as my spine lifts from the counter. Fuck, he's good at his task, and I can't stop writhing as the electric sparks sear every thought from my head.

He makes rumbling hums of pleasure as he sucks and licks the creamy coating from my body. It's all over his face, but he doesn't care. His tongue laps at my folds and sucks the dip off my clit with a thoroughness that has me tugging his hair, bucking and arching again in orgasm.

"Thor... god, I can't take anymore. Oh fuck," I whimper as he rubs his stubbly cheek against my thighs.

Thor flashes me a brief grin, then buries that clever tongue into my core, licking until I'm quivering and shrieking with the aftermath of another breath-stealing climax.

As I pant, chest heaving and thighs splayed, he smiles and snags a nearby kitchen towel from where it hangs on the stove to wipe his face. "Now that I've eaten you clean, it's your turn," he says, gripping his massive cock. Like a boneless doll, he turns me on the island, hanging my head off the side and fists my hair in one large hand.

Despite the languid satiation loosening my muscles, a thread of excitement flares to life. My mouth waters and I swallow. Neither Thor, Loki, or James have allowed me to suck their cocks over these past months since my characters invaded my life. Not that I've been with James more than once, and Thor has only visited a couple of times, but as often as Loki visits, like the others, he's always in control and I've barely gotten a chance to touch him. I'm certainly not going to waste the opportunity Thor is handing me. No way.

"Wait, I want dip, too," I say as I reach for the bowl. There is very little cheese dip left, but I pour the remainder into my hand as I reach for his flushed, dusky red cock with my free fingers.

Silk over rigid steel and like velvet to the touch. God, he's hot, almost burning in my palm. And so damn thick I can't circle him completely with my fingers. He throbs in my fingers as I stroke him to his base. His eyes gleam as I coat his length in the sticky, creamy dip, cock jerking at the cool concoction. With long flat strokes of my tongue, I lick and curl my tongue around him, starting at the base and working my way up the vein pulsing under my mouth. He groans as I get to the wide, flared head. My tongue explores every ridge, flicking over the little notched vee and swiping over the leaking pearly drops. I consume all the cheese, and then it's just him, the flavour of aroused male and that bite of ozone with a little salt before I attempt to stretch my mouth to suck him in.

Fuck, he's huge. His hand clenches in my hair, and I sense his restraint. My jaw aches trying to open enough to fit him into my mouth without catching my teeth on sensitive flesh.

"That's it, Melody. Open for me," he pants as he grips my chin with his other hand, pushing down to keep my jaw open.

It works. I relax into his hold, and his head glides back and forth over my lips and tongue. Using short thrusts, he sinks the first few inches in before hitting the back of my mouth, and I suck hard each time he pulls back. The taste of him has my mouth watering, and I close my eyes as saliva starts to trickle down my cheeks towards my eyes.

Unable to fit even close to his full length, I wrap both hands around his thick shaft, tugging in time with his hips as he fucks my mouth in short jerks that increase in tempo. My nipples peak and I squirm, rubbing my thighs together. As his groans grow louder, echoing through the kitchen, my pulse pounds with the rhythm of his thrusts. I reach a hand down to gently roll his balls.

"Fuck yes, do that!" he growls.

Pleasure ripples through my body as his voice deepens further, and his pace becomes more frenzied. Taking a single wet finger from his balls, I slide it behind until I can curl it just inside his ass to find that sensitive spot and apply pressure.

"*Fuck!*" he shouts, his body rigid, cock pushed to the back of my mouth.

Hot cum spurts, a geyser erupting in pulses. He tastes a bit salty, and a little metallic, almost like the lemon zinc vitamin C lozenges I suck on when I'm under the weather. He floods my mouth faster than I can swallow and some escapes my lips to coat my face, combining with the saliva smearing my skin.

Breathing heavily, Thor releases my hair to wipe the fluids out of my eyes and off my cheek with gentle fingertips. Opening sticky eyelashes, I gaze up at his wide smile as he withdraws from my mouth. Strong fingers carefully massage my jaw muscles as his lips twitch in amusement.

"You have a tiny little mouth, Melody."

"No Thor, you just have an enormous cock. I'm sure my mouth is normal-sized," I retort with a smirk.

He laughs and scoops me up off the counter. "Let's get you cleaned up. I'll help you make more dip for your friends since someone ate all of this and made a huge mess."

I snort with amusement even as he carries me upstairs to shower, washing my dip-smeared body and cum-streaked hair with a thoroughness that leaves me breathless. Okay, taking me up against the shower wall until I scream out my orgasm might also have something to do with why I'm breathless and weak in the knees when he helps me clean up the kitchen and put together new bowls of dip.

After a last kiss that sets my head spinning, he leaves, and I carry the food outside. I'm back in my sundress—miraculously unscathed by Thor's amorous attentions—with my wet hair piled up on my head with a clip.

"The burgers and dogs are ready," John calls out from the barbeque.

I set the dips down, and Nicole takes the veggie plate off the pile. She gives me a curious sidelong look, one eyebrow raised. "I went inside to help when you didn't come back for a while, and there was food smeared all over the island, but you weren't there. What happened?"

Oh fuck. Don't blush. Don't blush. *Don't blush!*

Shit. I'm totally blushing. My face is fiery red. I can feel it.

"Oh, ummm... I was having a case of klutziness, and the bowl spun right out of my hands, spilling everywhere. I had to go shower and clean up." My pulse pounds in my ears as I try not to squirm at my feeble lie.

She frowns, eyes flicking over my clean sundress and wet hair.

"Huh. That's so odd. I could have sworn I heard..." She shakes her head, then shrugs and reaches for some baby carrots. "Whatever. Let's eat!"

I let out a long, shaky exhale as my heart gradually slows its frantic thudding. Fuck. At least Loki didn't show up.

CHAPTER EIGHTEEN

All Tied Up

Half asleep after laying down in my hammock to sleep off the sangria effects when my friends left, I attempt to shift positions, but something holds my arm in place. Tugging, I can't move it. I grumble a complaint, my sleepy brain unable to figure out how I managed to pin my arm. I try to shift the other, and despite pulling, I can't move it either. Frustrated confusion drags me up from the depths of sleep to realize my legs are also pinned in place. Fighting against it, my eyes flutter open.

What the hell? This isn't a dream. I'm tied in place.

My heart lurches, then races, and I jerk my arms and legs frantically. The jingle of chain links has my lungs seizing as I tug desperately to get free and adrenaline surges.

A hand caresses my back from nape to ass, oddly calming my struggles, and a cool breeze tickles over my skin. Goosebumps break out over my flesh in a prickling ripple. I'm naked. Completely naked. What the everlasting hell is going on?

The hand strokes over me again in a light, but proprietary caress, and the pounding panic in my ears recedes further, allowing me to try to make sense of my situation.

Blinking at my surroundings, it takes me a minute to understand I'm suspended about three feet above the ground. Rough-spun cloth presses against my bare torso from below my breasts to my hips. It's holding me up. My head hangs down, and my hair blocks part of my vision, but by blowing the long strands out of my eyes, grass comes into view in front of me. Turning my head, there is my little pavilion with its wicker couches and behind it, my outdoor kitchen.

What the fuck? This is my yard.

With a hard swallow, I take in my situation. I'm suspended sideways in my hammock—padded cuffs at my wrists and ankles are linked to chains, keeping my arms and legs tied spread-eagle to the hammock stand frame. Who? Oh my god. Who has me? My pulse speeds again to pound like thunder in my ears, and my breath hiccups as another surge of adrenaline tightens my muscles, adding to my heightened senses.

Another long, lingering caress, but this time, the hand kneads an ass cheek. The stinging slap that follows has me jolting in shock and sucking in my breath. A fine trembling starts in my muscles as fear grips me.

A quiet rustling sound of footsteps over the short grass reaches my ears as the person behind me moves around, and black knee-length leather boots appear in my limited vision. Recognizing the distinctive footwear, relief rushes through my body. Tension leaves my muscles, along with a long, shaky, exhaled breath. A light-headed, dizzy sensation blurs my vision, and I close my eyes. As I relax into my suspended position, a heady sense of anticipation ignites in my abdomen. I don't know what he's got planned, but I know ultimately I'll enjoy it.

A hand grips the hair at the back of my head, stinging my scalp with a bite of pain as my head is lifted, and it swings my suspended body in an arc toward him. My eyes travel up long, leanly muscled thighs covered in black leather pants with a thick, rigid cock straining to break free, narrow hips and waist. Fine dark hairs just above the waistband disappear as my eyes move up the banded ridges of his bare muscled abdomen, only to reappear as a sprinkle of hairs on his chest with its little tight rosy nipples. Strong shoulders top off long arms of well-defined lean but powerful muscle.

I want to touch, to bury my nose in his skin, and lick my way up each muscular curve, then flick my tongue over sensitive nipples and dip it into the curve of his collarbone before trailing up that pale neck.

Higher up, an angular chin with that clever mouth, its rosy narrow lips currently turned up in a smirk. He knows I'm admiring the view, taking my time before meeting his eyes. A straight aristocratic nose is set between high, sharp cheekbones, raven-coloured curved brows framing brilliant green eyes with their long dark lashes. Those glittering eyes are narrowed, watching me with a darkly sinful menace, and my pulse leaps in response. Adrenaline and arousal blend into a heightened awareness to every touch of the breeze over my skin, the pain in my scalp at his hold, and his distinctive woodsy citrus and leather scent in my nose.

"What did I warn you about calling for me while another is fucking you, Melody?" His voice is eerily calm and silky smooth as he emphasizes each individual word in his sexy accent.

An icy sensation shivers down my spine at his tone and use of my name. Both are stark indications of the depths of possessive dominance I've roused in him. Fuck. I've fully woken the dangerous alpha male and can only hope to survive his animalistic instincts. Even as it scares me, making my pulse race in fluttery desperation and I arch my neck with instinctual submission, fiery arousal surges through my veins, drenching my core. Some part of me has wanted this, wanted to push him for months, and has been aching to have him show me exactly how savagely dominant he can be when he stakes his claim.

I lick my lips, cautious in my reply to the powerful god, my not-so-fictional character who has upended my understanding of reality. "That... that it would make you lose control."

His voice drops lower and quieter, menace dripping from his tone as he replies, "And what would happen to you when I lost control?"

"You would..." I pause to lick my lips again as my breath rasps in airy little pants. "You would thoroughly fuck me, claim me, brand my body as yours, so I'd never doubt it again."

His eyes lock on mine, and I'm unable to look away. "So you understand what's about to happen? I need to hear you say it."

I tremble, fine shivers rippling over my body. "Yes, Loki."

A pleased expression flits over his face before the unholy light of erotic danger overtakes his features once again. "Good girl. Give me a safe word. I won't be stopping to ask if you are okay this time, so I have to trust you will use it if you need me to stop."

"Red," I manage to squeak.

Chapter Nineteen

His Promise

Loki's lips stretch into a slow, evil smile as he frees his straining cock from his pants. "Let's see if I can shove my cock further down your throat than Thor did, shall we? Unlike him, I'm not going to be nice and gentle. If you need me to stop, snap your fingers."

His words send a shiver over my skin. With the hand in my hair, he directs my mouth to the broad head, painting my lips with glittering pearly droplets. I flick my tongue out to trace over the slit. It's hot, tasting of warm male and leather. I've wanted to taste him for months now, and he's put me off, taking me in other ways instead. He's always in control, and I've hardly been allowed to get my hands on him. I can hardly believe I'm getting both him and Thor in the same day.

After opening my mouth eagerly, he teases me with short thrusts that barely let his head enter, sliding on my tongue. I can't move my head at all. He's got me firmly in his grip and sets the pace, but I curl my tongue around him, flicking over the little vee every time he retreats.

He hisses in reaction. "You've got a clever tongue in that wet little mouth of yours," he grunts, sinking deeper into my mouth, almost to the back.

I hum, and he shoves further, hitting my gag reflex, staying deep.

"Swallow and open your jaw, little one. You are going to take me deeper still."

As I obediently swallow against the thick obstruction, he delves further with each movement of my throat, until my face rests against the dark curly hairs at the base of his cock. My lungs scream for air, that I need to breathe, but I fight the instinctive panic against choking. I've never held a cock this deep into my throat before. God, I can hardly believe I've managed it now. His eyes glow with approval, and it helps me relax against my instincts.

"I do love the look of those pink lips of yours stretched so wide around my cock."

A hum is my only answer.

His free hand caresses my cheek, eyes dark with lust even as he holds himself buried in my throat. "Remember to take a quick breath in as I pull out. I don't want you passing out as I fuck this hot little mouth of yours. I'm not going to stop ravaging it until my cum pours down your throat and spills out your soft, sexy lips."

No sooner does he warn me than he withdraws until he's poised at my lips. Already feeling a little lightheaded, I take a couple of quick breaths through my nose. A little fear keeps my pulse racing, yet arousal swirls hotly with my body. Flickers of electricity spark along nerve endings.

With a dark, possessive look, he plunges back in, hitting my throat, causing me to gag and swallow as he presses until he's completely seated. He pauses for a couple of seconds while my throat convulses around him, groaning.

Pulling back, he sets a slow rhythm of in, pause as I swallow, then out again.

"Fuck, your mouth feels so bloody good," he growls, increasing his pace.

Saliva spills, coating my chin and starting to form strings falling to the grass below. The carnal plunder of my mouth as he shoves his cock deep, hair wrapped in his tight fist on the back of my head to keep me exactly where he wants me, has my body tingling with prickly heat, concentrating between my thighs. My nipples pebble into hard nubs, and moisture trickles from my sex.

"This is my fucking mouth, do you hear me, little writer? *Mine*. You are going to feel my cock plundering your little throat every time you try to talk. Every time you try to swallow. Every time you breathe, you are going to remember this feeling. Every time you fucking eat or drink, you are going to taste me on your lips and tongue," he snarls as his thrusts get harder, faster, rougher, and more raw. "*Mine* to fuck. *Mine* to destroy."

The lightheaded sensation expands and I start to float, with only sipped gasps of air, my chances to breathe, but I don't want him to stop. As contrary as it is, a sense of power grows within me at his loss of control, as his thighs begin to shake and his growls of pleasure get louder. Both of his hands are in my hair now, clasping and unclasping into fists that tug, and nails that scrape against my scalp.

His body locks, spine rigid, and with a roar of sound, he releases. Pressing his cock as deep as it will go, the hot flood pours down my throat, and I swallow over and over.

Withdrawing as his cock continues to twitch, the last spurts hit my tongue. It's both slightly sweet and salty, but also tart, like salted caramel popcorn and lemon zest. Breathing heavily, his hands massage my scalp as I lick my lips. I can't do anything about the saliva and other fluids coating my chin.

Awareness dawns that I'm panting, too. Not just from catching my breath, but also from the carnal need coursing through my body. My core throbs with a second heartbeat, and my nipples ache to be touched. It's a fire in my blood, scorching me from the inside out.

Loki's eyes burn with naked savage desire as he looks down at my face. Still hard, he's completely ready for more, as if I needed further evidence of his stamina. Combining those traits of the trickster, storyteller, and fertility god seemed good at the time when I outlined his character traits, but damn, he's far surpassed what I'd envisioned. Taking my chin with one hand and gripping my hair with the other, he tilts me up higher and captures my mouth in a hard, possessive kiss. His tongue delves and strokes, demanding my surrender and pulling a whimpered moan of need from me.

A rumbled low growl escapes him as our lips part. "You don't think I'm done with you yet, do you?"

"God, I hope not!" I moan.

A slow, seductive smile stretches his lips. "Good answer," he purrs.

He swings my body up further and his mouth latches onto a taut nipple. A wail of need escapes me. The strong suckling pulls from the center of my body like he's drawing out my soul. I can't help but writhe as he moves between my breasts. Warmth flows from my center, expanding outward, and my hips buck with my increasing desire.

After releasing my nipple with a scrape of his teeth, he lets my body swing back down and prowls around me. The breeze caresses aching flesh, left wet from his mouth. I shiver at the cool sensation against my overheated skin.

Although I can't see Loki, I know he's behind me. I sense his presence, like a blazing inferno waiting to burn me with the force of his desire, even if he isn't touching me yet. I tug my legs—my nerves getting the better of me—but there is no give in the bindings he's used, and my body simply sways on the fabric sling of hammock material.

"Isn't this a beautiful sight," he purrs. Long fingers grip my ass cheeks, kneading. "You are flushed and dripping, my little writer. Positively drenched and aching for me."

His words send a bolt of heat surging through me, and I squirm my hips in his grasp. Tilting me back towards him, I jerk as his tongue strokes over my clit and my sex, dipping in, only to continue to my ass.

A long moan escapes my lips. It's like being stroked by lightning. Internally, I wince. Damn good thing I didn't say *that* out loud with his current mood.

"Please, Loki. More," I beg, aching and desperate.

"Do you need to cum?" he purrs as he licks me again in a long, sensuous stroke and my muscles quiver, my abdomen a heated coil.

"Yes! Please, Loki!"

"Oh no, Melody. You've been a very, very bad little writer." His voice deepens into a rough erotic snarl as pain explodes on my ass from a hard slap.

I suck in a sharp breath. "Oh, fuck."

The sting heats my skin and sinks into the warmth flowing in my core as he continues to talk. "This sexy little body is *mine* to do with what I want..."

Another stinging slap has me gasping. "Fuck."

"And what I want is to fill all your tight little holes with my cum, to cover you in my scent, to brand your body from the inside so you never, *ever* doubt who you belong to." Each of his points is punctuated by hard slaps on my ass cheeks and the backs of my thighs.

I can't help but groan at the delicious warmth heating my core from his primal words and spanking. "Oh, fuck."

"You are mine, and I'm going to punish this soaked, needy little cunt and tiny tight ass with my big cock," he snarls, impaling my pussy on his cock in one hard thrust that seats him right to the root.

"*Fuck!*" I scream, my inner walls pulsing with shock at the sudden invasion. Pain, pleasure—god, I can't tell with my nerves snapping like firecrackers.

He slowly withdraws.

I whine at the loss. "No... please, Loki."

He aims a stinging slap to my clit, drawing my shriek as the fiery pain shifts to searing arousal.

"God!"

Again, he drives his cock deep, to the hilt, and a wail escapes my lips at the shocking, delicious fullness. "*Oh my god!*"

His voice is a threatening growl when he withdraws to slap my pussy again. "Only when you are overflowing with my cum, completely mindless with need, will I allow you to climax. I own and control your pleasure. It belongs to *me*. Then, and only then, will I keep you cumming until your fragile, little human body passes out from too much pleasure. That is my promise to you, little writer."

My ass and pussy burn, aching from the repeated slaps and teasing single thrusts as he continues until I shake with need.

"Please! Loki, please fuck me," I plead, uncaring that I'm begging. Whatever he wants, he can have if he'll just fuck me, just satisfy the fire burning me from the inside out.

"You won't be able to sit without feeling me," he snarls.

He's unrelenting, continuing to inflame my body and mind with stinging slaps on my ass, thighs, and pussy, with those single, violent penetrating thrusts of his cock. Never enough to send me over. Just enough to keep me poised on the blade's edge. It's heaven and hell combined. Perfectly full when he's inside, yet so empty when he draws his rigid length out each time, leaving me aching for that undeniable connection to him.

My face is hot and tears sting my eyes at the confusion of my senses.

"*Please*, Loki!"

Every part of my sex is inflamed. My pulse thumps with a second heartbeat in my swollen clit and plumped lips.

"You are so incredibly beautiful like this," he growls as slams his cock into my drenched pussy to the tune of my shriek.

Strong hands grip my hips as he pistons in and out with rapid, rough thrusts that have me howling in ecstasy. It tingles up my spine, burning down my legs, coiling in my core. I gasp and whimper at the strength of the rising inferno.

"Don't you dare fucking cum, little writer," Loki snarls as the walls of my pussy start to tremble.

I'm on the precipice. So close. God, I'm so close.

"I can't stop it!" I gasp.

Chapter Twenty

Claimed

Loki reaches a hand up to my head even as his hips continue to slam against me, the impact hitting my clit each time. Delicious sparks flare with every contact.

"You *will not* cum until I allow it!"

His power wraps around my nerves, keeping me at the threshold, pinned like a butterfly fluttering madly on a board. It's agony, but such ecstasy at the same time.

"*Loki!*" I plead desperately. The need is a towering firestorm in my blood.

"*No!* You are *mine* and you will cum when I say so!" he growls, even as he shouts his own release, the hot flood filling me in a surge.

He stays buried, still hard and demanding, as he catches his breath.

I writhe, trying to squirm, to get the punishing friction I crave. I want more. God, I need more. It's making me frantic, breath rasping in harsh gasps, as tears stream down my face.

"Still up for more, are you?" his voice holds amusement at my predicament.

"Please, Loki. Please let me cum?" I whine like the needy little submissive he's drawn out of me. I don't care. My entire focus is on the flames within me, the need searing my flesh.

He withdraws his cock, and I whine louder, eliciting a chuckle from Loki. "Getting desperate, little one?"

"Yes," I moan. No part of me wants to deny it in the slightest. I'll do whatever he wants, whatever he demands, if he'll just satisfy this relentless fire in my veins that's turned me mindless.

Something cold touches my ass, contrasting against my hot skin, and I flinch before I realize what it is. Loki spreads it over my back entrance, circling, before pushing a slippery finger in.

"Unless you want me to rip you apart, you need to relax this tight little ass. Push out now," he commands in a low purr.

I obey—my body a churning mass of scorching need.

More cold hits my fiery flesh and he inserts a second finger, slowly moving them in and out as he keeps adding the chilled lube.

I shiver at the erotic caress and stark contrast of cold with my heated body. Both sensations add fuel to the already raging inferno inside me.

"You have until I cum in this little cunt of yours again to relax this sexy tight ass, because ready or not, my big cock will be fucking it shortly," he growls as he slams his cock inside my pussy again, thrusting at a rapid pace as his two long fingers scissor and stretch my ass.

"Oh god... god... Loki!" I shriek, trembling, body bucking as his power prevents me from cumming, despite the overwhelming blaze igniting my veins in powerful bursts. It's hard to think. All I can do is feel. Shaking my head, I'm mindless to anything else.

"Whose little cunt is this?" he demands, each hard stroke slamming against my clit as he bottoms out in my pussy.

"Yours, Loki," I whimper.

"I can't hear you. Whose?" he snarls, pounding harder and faster.

"*Yours*, Loki!" I howl, trembling, needy whines escaping my throat with each body-shaking impact. God, I never want him to stop. Never... never... never. Each thrust strums every pleasurable nerve within me as tears stream from my closed eyes. Every ounce of my concentration is focused on the fiery sensations flaring from my lower body.

His body turns rigid, then he shouts as his hips jerk. His cock releases in hot pulses against my cervix. Moaning at the loss of the pounding thrusts, I squirm, pinned on the throbbing cock inside me.

Still pulsing when he withdraws from my pussy, his cock pushes with relentless pressure against my ass. It feels enormous, so much wider than his fingers. Fear shivers up my spine in an involuntary cold stroke, like ice along my back. Breathing hard through my nose, I clench my teeth as I attempt to will my lower body to relax.

I want this, even as it scares me.

The head pops through the ring of muscle with a suddenness I'm not expecting, and I jolt, keening at the painful, stretching penetration. With my hands clenching at the chains, my breath comes in little puffs, flaring my nostrils. Desperately, I try to adjust to the unfamiliar fullness.

Oh god. Do I still want this? The heat in my veins mixes with the cold on my spine, swirling in an uncertain brew within me.

Loki groans, a long, low rumble of sound. With steady pressure, he penetrates deeper, expanding that biting stretch until his hips meet my ass. Fuck. He feels so much larger, and I'm panting, not sure if I want him there or not. He leans over my back, one hand twisting my hair around his fist while his other curls around my throat from the front. He tilts me up and back, his chest pressed tight to my back, with his mouth near my ear.

The heat from his body sears my senses, chasing away the chill. Held so tightly, dominated so fully, the bite of pain blends, shifting into fuel for the inferno inside me. As contradictory as it is, his unrelenting hold flips the last of the resistance within me, letting me submit to his power. Safe to release myself into his care, I relax.

"Do you feel how tight your little ass is squeezing my cock? I'm going to fuck you so hard and so deep, you are going to see entire galaxies of stars," he purrs into my ear in a low, sensual growl.

His hips start to move in long, smooth strokes as he's talking, and my mouth drops open at the intensely dirty and sinful feel of his cock moving in my ass. It's shocking and insanely satisfying. Holy fuck, I never want him to stop.

"You like that, don't you... the feel of my thick cock fucking your tiny ass?" His voice shivers down my spine like a physical stroke, even as the sensation of his thrusting cock sends flames cascading up to meet and explode like sparks spit from a fire in my clit and nipples. "Answer me," he demands.

I moan, a long drawn-out guttural sound at the base of my throat as I try to respond. My mind is a swirling maelstrom of sensation, and I'm not sure if I manage to say any actual words or not.

"Answer me, little writer," he demands as his hips move faster, and the hand at my throat squeezes.

"*Yes*," I keen, bucking at the fiery heat searing my nerve endings as it builds and expands, moving out from where his hips slam into my ass, scorching my flesh with each possessive thrust.

Loki growls against my neck as he fucks me, holding me tightly in place for every punishing stroke, as I beg for him to let me cum. I can't even toss my head with his fierce grip on my hair. Impaled on the sharp spikes of desire he's built within me, I plead for release.

"Whose sexy little ass is this?" he snarls into my ear.

"Yours, Loki," I sob.

"That's right. It's mine. Like this little cunt and this smart mouth of yours that I fucked and filled with my seed.

It's all mine. Now *cum*," he snarls, then bites the tender spot where my shoulder and neck meet.

The explosive force of a nuclear detonation rips me apart. Starbursts of light explode behind my eyes. I can't see. Some part of me recognizes I'm screaming, but I can't hear it. I only sense the violent thrashing of my body against the tight restraint of Loki's grip. In pulsing waves, I'm shattered and remade, over, and over, and over.

Loki roars, and his cock spurts, yet he snarls and continues fucking me right through his orgasm, forcing mine to continue. Just as I think it's finished, another powerful explosion blasts through me, and I writhe in helpless reaction.

Again.

And again

And again.

And still again.

Through it all, Loki continues to growl against the base of my neck, teeth clamped on as he fucks me, hips slamming against my ass, his cock hard and unrelenting in its demand that I cum repeatedly. It's a raw, primitive fucking that wrings me out completely.

I lose track, one orgasm blending into the next, until I'm limp, floating and unable to respond to the explosive bursts with more than a weak shudder. My head is entirely held up by Loki's hand in my hair and at my neck. My eyes shut, too tired to remain open. A weak mewling is all that emerges from my exhausted throat by the time Loki cums again for the fourth or fifth time since my orgasms started.

I've lost count.

I'm a sweaty, sticky mess, covered in his scent and seed, with it dripping off my body. His breath is hot against my neck as he kisses and licks my skin. It's the last thing I remember, as my mind decides it's had enough.

CHAPTER TWENTY-ONE

This Is Your Wake-Up Call

Something wakes me. Some instinct telling me I'm not alone. I don't want to be awake yet. It can't possibly be time to get up. Blurrily, I open my eyes and look over at the clock.

7:15 am

Nope, I definitely do not want to be awake yet. Fuck's sake, I went to sleep around two in the morning after drinking too much caffeine again while writing. I scrunch my eyes closed and pull the soft, blue blanket under my chin as I curl tighter on my left side, but I can't quite fall asleep.

Heat seeps through the covers against my back. I roll slightly towards it and encounter resistance. More resistance than there should be from my body pillow. Harder, firmer, and immovable.

I tilt back until I'm pressed fully against it, confirming my suspicions. I groan slightly, sure of what I'll find when I open my eyes. It is Friday morning, after all. The day I post a new chapter of *Hidden* to my beta-readers.

If I don't open my eyes, he's not there, right? I can get a few more hours of sleep?

"You might as well open your eyes, little writer. I know you are awake," a sensuous accent purrs.

I pull the sheet over my face, and a low chuckle vibrates the warm chest I'm leaning against.

"But I don't want to get up yet. I'm tired," I complain, even as I blink.

The sheet is tugged off my face by two long white fingers hooked over the edge, and I turn my face to see him peering down at me, amusement on those narrow lips, quirked in a half smile. Black hair falls over part of his face, and I meet his green eyes. You would think I would be used to the impact of his gorgeous features by now, but no, my heart jolts in my chest just as it did the first time he visited me.

Every time he visits me.

As his eyebrow lifts in question, his fingers grip my chin with casual, relentless strength. "Do you need help waking this morning?"

"Huh?" Not my most intelligent response as a writer, but please, I *am* still waking up.

His eyes darken with intent. "Do you need help waking this morning?" he says slower, emphasizing each word.

I squeak. Yes, I absolutely squeak, and my heart is now thudding a rapid tattoo. "No!" I shake my head. "Nope, no help needed. I'll get up, Loki."

He gazes at me without response for a long minute, and I'm frozen in place, shallow breaths making me lightheaded. I know what the rabbit feels like before the cougar pounces as I wait for him to decide. And in my case, he's fully capable of shifting to that woman-eating three-hundred-pound panther as he did in the years he spent as the Egyptian goddess Bastet and Aztec god Tezcatlipoca.

It's not that he'll hurt me in any way I won't like. Oh no. Not at all. You know death is not what I mean by woman-eating. Unless you are thinking *la petite mort*, the little death. He's always been a sex god, regardless of which gender he presents as.

No, the problem is I like it too much, and when Loki gets his way, I lose hours, sometimes days, of writing time. It completely wipes me out. Endorphin overload. I don't have his stamina.

I'm only human, after all. Not an immortal. Not a god. Certainly not a fertility god like he is.

I need more recovery time, damn it.

When Loki let his possessive nature take over to claim every part of me in an overwhelming dominance display of sexual prowess—while earth-shattering and not *ever* an experience I'll forget—it also had me uncomfortable and sitting carefully for the next four days. And that was after I woke from the orgasm coma that knocked me out for a full day.

I'm still slightly on the tender side a week later.

Perhaps if he wasn't quite so well-endowed, I'd recover faster from his vigorous fucking. But then, given how amazing he feels inside me, the friction that is the perfect blend of fullness and just this side of too much, I wouldn't want him any different. Nope, he's perfect, but don't tell him that. His ego does not need any additional stroking.

Some of it is certainly my fault. I just can't resist asking him to pound me harder and faster. It drives me absolutely crazy every single time, and I cum so hard I see stars. Literally, stars. Entire fucking galaxies.

Totally worth it.

Although, perhaps the *next* time Loki fucks me into submission for deliberately making him jealous, I need to gag myself before I beg for more? I really am a glutton for punishment, but I mean, come on. Do you really blame me? I'm amazed I stayed conscious as long as I did with the overwhelming orgasms he gave me once he allowed me to cum.

Did I mention he's a bit of a control freak in the bedroom? Don't tell him, but he's not wrong. I never cum so hard as when he forces me to wait. I may yell and curse him at the time, but he knows exactly what he's doing. He plays my body like the virtuoso he is.

Damn him.

"Are you still sore, little writer?" he finally asks quietly, his hand warm on my chin.

I look away, unable to hold his gaze as my cheeks flush with heat. "A little."

His fingers caress my cheek. "I need to be a little less vigorous with you, and not forget myself, even when you beg so nicely. You seem to have no self-preservation once I get my cock in you."

My eyes flick to his to see the humour and heat in them.

I'd never really considered myself submissive in the bedroom, but that dominant, slightly dangerous vibe Loki gives off has me complying with whatever he wants, whenever he wants it. Even taking my ass hard and deep for the first time in a savage display that blew my mind and body. He always ensures I am perfectly safe and entirely enthusiastic, even as I tease him by playing reluctant or bratty. I completely trust that he'll guarantee I enjoy myself. Just as he trusts I'll tell him if it edges from pleasurable pain to true pain.

And there hadn't been any actual pain, despite his threatening talk and rough handling. I love his threatening, dirty talk. It drives me crazy. And I definitely don't mind bruises and achy muscle soreness for a few days as a trade-off for mind-blowing orgasms.

Again, totally worth it.

Shifting position to get up, my weight against him no impediment to his strength, he tosses the blankets off me and scoops me into his arms. The sound of water pouring into the two-person soaker tub starts in the bathroom. "I'm taking care of you this morning," he states, his tone telling me not to argue as he carries me.

With a smile, I loop my arms around his neck and tuck my head into his neck. He smells so good. I can't help but lick up the side of his warm skin, tasting him. Woody citrus and warm male. Yum.

"Behave, or it will be a cold shower for you," he threatens, voice dropping low as he sets me on my feet on the white bathroom tile.

He's been like this since I woke from my orgasm coma, insisting on caring for me by bathing me, brushing my hair, and rubbing healing cream on my bruised ass and thighs. Of course, that gets me all hot and wet, but he flatly refuses to do anything until I'm no longer tender and sore. It frustrated me enough that I'd insisted I was fine to take care of myself yesterday.

He didn't like that at all.

Neither did I, actually. I missed him, but I was too stubborn to call for him after I'd let my pride drive him away. Clearly, I'm stupid sometimes.

After all, parts of me are just fine and craving his touch, thank you very much, even if I still have the shape of Loki's hands imprinted on my ass.

I know better than to try to win that argument, though. Loki has a will of iron when it comes to deciding when and how he's going to play with my body. I'm still too sore to attempt to break his control by getting him jealous again. If I can't handle the consequences, I'm not foolish enough to tempt him. I suspect his fury if he hurt me in truth because I didn't know my limits, would be truly traumatic for both of us.

Especially when it's the consequences I want.

I'll wait until the rest of the bruising fades, and I can sit without wincing before I incite more. God, it was so totally worth it. I'll be poking the dangerous panther again at some point, possibly sooner than is wise. He's just so incredibly, insanely fucking hot when he loses it!

"Fine," I retort a bit petulantly. When he raises a single eyebrow, I know I'm pushing it. Damn, but he can say a lot without ever saying a word.

"Will you take your clothes off, or should I?"

The threat hangs in the air. If he takes them off, they'll be destroyed, and I am wearing my favourite sleep shirt. I quickly whip it over my head and slide my panties off.

He chuckles as he gets rid of his own.

As tempted as I am to make a smart-ass comment to assuage my pride stinging from his humour at how fast I obeyed him, it won't end well for me if I do. I bite my lip to not respond to the clear taunt.

Who says I'm not a fast learner?

CHAPTER TWENTY-TWO

Aftercare

With a little half-smile on his lips, he turns me to face away from him. His fingers are gentle as he probes my ass and thighs, watching my reaction. Is he wanting to see if I flinch? In the mirror over the double sinks, I can see the ones on my thighs are faint smudges. They don't hurt at all. Same with those higher up on my ass. It's only the ones where my ass and thigh meet that are still a bit painful to the touch.

Satisfied with his assessment, he scoops me in his arms to step into the tub and sits with me cradled on his lap. Even in my annoyance, I appreciate he's got his strong thighs spread to create a pocket for my hips that keeps the worst of my bruised ass off the hard bottom of the tub.

The hot water slowly creeps up his thighs as the level deepens, but hasn't yet reached me. I lean back against his warm chest and turn my head to listen to his strong heartbeat. His arm is around my waist, pinning me to him.

But I know what he's doing.

He's ensuring I can't raise myself to sit on the hard cock poking me in the lower back, while his other hand plays with my hair. Nor is it possible for me to reach with my fingers. It is so tempting, though. Hot steel branding my back and stirring heat in my core. I really want to.

He knows it, too, damn it.

I sigh, unable to keep the slight pout from my lips, as I let my fingers trace circles over his muscular forearm. Soft, dark hairs cover his pale skin in a gorgeous study of contrasts.

Loki's chest shakes as he chuckles. "Are you feeling frustrated, little writer?" He gives a lock of my hair a little playful tug.

"Yes," I sigh again, unable to keep from shifting restlessly with the arousal I always experience around Loki, even when he's doing nothing to intentionally stir me up. I crave him. He's like a drug in my veins.

"Well, we can't have that, now can we?" he says, his voice dropping to a seductive purr.

I'm not expecting it at all when his hands grasp my hips to shift me so the water pouring from the tap suddenly bombards my clit.

"*Holy shit!*" I shriek as the relentless water pressure pounds, and I flail for something to hold on to. The orgasm is sharp, fast, and furious, exploding over my senses like a soap bubble expanding, then losing cohesion in a burst.

When Loki returns me to his chest, I'm shaking and gasping for breath. My heart races from the insane speed of my climax.

"That was effective," he purrs against my ear.

I relax into him, boneless. It takes me a minute to notice, with my nerves buzzing, that he's got one hand lightly tracing over my still spasming clit, and the other tugging one peaked nipple.

"Are you still frustrated?" he asks as his fingertips delve lightly through my wet folds.

"What... what if I am?" I ask between ragged breaths. Like I'm going to turn him down? No way!

His fingers press more firmly along my folds, watching my face intently.

What is he looking for? Oh... he's testing to see if I have any lingering bruising here from the spanking he'd given me. As an expanding warmth from his tender care wakes every cell of my body, I smile. "My pussy isn't sore, Loki. It's just the bruises on my ass that are left—" My sentence ends with a long moan as his fingers curl inside to stroke over my G-spot.

By the gods, he knows exactly how to finger me. My eyes roll back and I squirm as the sensation builds. His thumb continues to slide against and press my clit as his fingers work me. My pelvis tingles, prickling with sparking heat.

Pressure grows, intensifying, like steam trapped in a pipe. Fuck, it's hotter with each stroke of his fingers. My hips buck until I'm rigid, my spine arched.

"*Loki!*" I yell as the pressure bursts. Electricity rips up my back to explode in my head, and a gush of fluid covers his fingers, coating my thighs.

"Mmm... next time I make you squirt, I want it in my mouth," Loki growls, sucking his fingers.

Lifting me, he lays my back on the wide platform surrounding the tub, with my hips suspended out over the water. Widening my legs, he lowers his head, groaning as he draws his tongue over my inner thighs.

"Such a feast you are, little one. I'll never tire of your taste," he says before sucking the sensitive skin of both inner thighs, then licking long strokes over my drenched and heated core. Delving deep with his tongue, only to circle and tease, he varies his strokes between firm stabs and long, flat laps. He seals his lips around my clit, sucking hard while his tongue flicks, driving me hard and fast into another spine-tingling orgasm.

I'm panting, trembling as he slows his pace, releases my clit, and laps at my core again in long, slow strokes. Taking his time, he kisses my thighs and moves up my abdomen, letting my breathing calm and my heart rate return to a more reasonable rhythm compared to its earlier desperate tempo.

"Better, my little writer? I wouldn't want you to think I wasn't taking proper care of you." His hands glide over my skin in long, massaging caresses as he glances up from pressing kisses to my abdomen.

"Definitely," I agree, scraping the fingertips of one hand across his scalp. I love the feeling of his thick hair, silky between my fingers.

His eyelids lower, and I know he's enjoying it.

With his effortless strength, he lifts me off the edge of the tub and lays me face down on his chest in the hot water. He tucks my head into his shoulder, keeping my hand in his hair. As I continue to play with his hair, I nuzzle against his neck, kissing the skin, and pulling in his scent. Being surrounded by him... it settles something deep within me. Even if I fall asleep, I know I can relax and he'll keep me safe.

At some point, he turned off the hot water when I was distracted. With both of us in the tub, it's deep enough now to cover our chests. He cups the water to bring it up my back, letting it pour down from his hand, over and over.

"Mmm... Loki?"

"Yes?"

"Why do you enjoy taking care of me like this?"

His hand pauses in releasing the water on my nape. "Why wouldn't I? I have your curvy little body naked and draped over me."

The water trickles from his hand and down my skin. Tilting my head, I gaze up at his face to see his lips curve, a mix of pleasure and amusement in his half-lidded green eyes.

"You want to know what I'm thinking and feeling, don't you, my curious little one? Trying to get further into my head?" he purrs, even as his grin stretches wider.

Actually, that isn't my motivation, but the truth would leave me too vulnerable. After all, he only visits me because he wants to ensure that the stories I tell with him as a character accurately reflect his reality. I'd willingly agreed to the trade of smoking hot sex for access to his insights.

"Always," I agree.

"Very well." His hand slides down my back again. "The heat of the water feels good, relaxing, but nowhere near as perfect as the heat from your body against me. Your skin is so soft and fragile compared to mine, and although I don't want you in pain, I'm finding the sight of the bruises I've left on your sexy ass arousing and satisfying in a very animalistic way." His fingertips lightly trace over the marks as he looks down my body.

"Yes, I'll definitely be leaving my mark on your skin in the future." A rumbling sound vibrates his chest, and gazing into his eyes, the glow of banked desire illuminates the green depths. "What else? Your body is relaxed, pliant and sultry curves, whereas I'm all hard angles. The contrast inspires thoughts of exploring and sinking into your soft, wet heat."

He tilts his head down, almost touching my lips, but not quite. "Your breath tickles over my skin, and your heartbeat speeds, like it just did now. As I play with your level of arousal, your pupils dilate. Your responsiveness is enchanting and never fails to increase my own desire for you."

My hand tightens in his hair, tugging his head towards me so I can kiss him.

His eyes gleam, resisting the movement for a second, just to show me he can, before he presses his lips to mine. Softly, he kisses me in teasingly light touches. His tongue traces the seam of my lips before slipping inside in a slow, sensual exploration.

It draws a moan out of me, even as I tremble at his tender touches. My eyes flutter open to look into his when he pulls his head back, parting our lips.

One side of his mouth quirks, and he shifts me down his body to slowly impale me on his cock.

"Oh god. Loki. God," I whimper at the invasion.

The stretching fullness has my core tingling and quivering. I try to push down to hurry the achingly slow penetration, but Loki's strength completely defeats my efforts. Even once he's buried to the base, he doesn't speed up his withdrawing stroke or the next as he sinks back inside.

The unhurried, gentle seduction has my muscles shuddering and my thoughts scattering.

The sensual purr of his voice pulls me from the pleasurable haze overtaking my mind with his leisurely plundering of my body. "You are strong-willed and confident, yet you allow yourself to be completely vulnerable to me like this. I find that trust and surrender, allowing me to do what I want with you, to be extremely enticing, gratifying, and provocative. Your submission pulls at my instincts and desires. It makes me want to reward you, even as I fulfill a deep-seated need to possess you, control your pleasure, and see those beautiful eyes go blind as you writhe and moan your climax when I allow it. It satisfies my primal chaotic nature to hear the sounds you make, the helpless clenching of your wet little cunt, and the flush of arousal over your skin."

My only response to his words is a long, drawn-out keen. I'm too caught up in pleasurable torment as he holds me in place. I'm writhing. Panting. Pinned in place on his cock that continues its tortuously slow strokes in and out.

His smile widens. "Yes, exactly like that. I can feel how close you are, your little walls quivering desperately around my cock. I know how much you love it when I pound you hard, fast, and deep, but slow and thorough is sometimes exactly—"

His words, in that low sensual purr, with the imagery and memory it evokes, have my spine arching and my entire body bucking in Loki's hands as the orgasm ignites and flashes through me.

Loki groans, his own body jerking. "Damn, woman. Your tight, needy little cunt milked the cum right out of me."

Collapsing bonelessly on his chest, I pant, listening to his thumping heartbeat. The rhythm is soothing. His chest vibrates as he laughs, and I look up to meet his gaze.

He leans down to kiss me gently. "Did I answer your question adequately, little writer? Suffice it to say, you have me wrapped around your finger just as deeply as my cock is buried in your cunt." His hands massage the muscles of my back, finding every knot that needs relaxation.

It's heavenly. Like a cat, I'm curled up on him, absolutely enjoying every pampering stroke of his hands.

"Mmm... yes, for now. I'm sure I'll have more for you later," I tease, and he smirks, stilling my chuckle with another kiss.

Ladies' Night

Episode Four Description

When Loki invades not just my reality but threatens my heart, this writer distracts herself with a night on the town.

***

Inviting a few of my fictional characters to let loose at Club Illusion seems like a great idea to get my mind off Asgard's Black Prince. After all, ladies' night means no men, so no distracting god that has me questioning my sanity. It's one thing to deal with his growly possession and sexy talk that melt the panties right off me, but I can't risk unlocking my heart. He's not for me and I know it. But Loki is a trickster for a reason. I may have underestimated the lengths Loki will go to when he wants to play dirty.

CHAPTER TWENTY-THREE

Escaping To Club Illusion

Have I lost my mind? Pausing with my mascara wand in hand, I stare at my reflection in the harsh white lights of my ensuite bathroom, then shrug. Maybe... It's a reasonable question considering the line between what I've always believed to be the real world and my imaginary worlds has shattered into glittering shards of my former plane of existence.

My nose wrinkles as I lean away from the silver surface, lowering the wand.

Even if I could rebuild those walls between universes, I wouldn't want to return to my previous naive state. Life was empty, spent rattling around my grandmother's house after her death and uncertain about what to do with myself. Writing, and all the experiences that have come with my new career, have saved me. Well, saved me for now. The woman in the mirror winces and my sigh echoes off the white tile and cream-coloured walls of the bathroom.

Better enjoy this thrilling ride for as long as I can.

While blowing a kiss at myself, I wink at my reflection's knowing grin, lean in and finish applying my mascara. There's no denying that of late, I spend more time with my fictional characters than with friends from my world. I'm just not that close to anyone here anymore, not for the last three years. It's hard to get past the knowledge that my 'real world' friends knew my now ex-boyfriend was cheating on me and didn't clue me in. Hanging out with them occasionally has been as much as I can seem to manage.

And my fictional characters have yet to let me down. I have so much fun with them. Maybe I'm embracing chaos by doing so, but I've invited Shannon, Kara, and Mist to come out with me for a night on the town. A clear sign of my descent into madness, but really, what's the worst that can happen? They disappear in front of others? They start some trouble and leave me to deal with it? My laugh fills the space of the bathroom as I add eyeshadow.

Hell, it's not like I can even send them back to their fictional universe with a hangover. It would instantaneously dissipate when they cross the barrier between realities since they pop right back into their story timeline from the last point that I've sent a chapter to beta-readers.

And other things don't seem to come through, either.

Discovering Shannon isn't pregnant when she comes here to visit?! I shake my head and lower the make-up brush in my fingers. Now, *that* was a jaw-dropper. Where does the baby go in the interim? Bizarrely, it's like nothing that happens here affects their reality. They only recall this reality when they hear my call to cross over, then their memory of events here returns. It's mind-boggling.

Every time I've pondered these conundrums, I go in circles. I can't work out the paranormal mechanics. These kinds of things could drive an author absolutely bonkers. With a glance back up, I check out the smoky blues and silver eyeshadow highlighting my hazel eyes, then dig out my red lip stain from the open drawer. Ha, maybe I already am crackers, considering how much time I spend with my characters.

But they just don't feel fictional to me anymore.

Not since Loki invaded my world and brought the rest with him.

Maybe if I shift to writing pure science fiction, I'll need to better understand all the ins and outs of inter-dimensional travel, instead of the science-fantasy and conspiracy thriller romance I write now.

My reflection cocks her head. Does he understand how it works? I roll my eyes at myself, then apply the lip stain. Loki seems to be well-travelled and co-exists as multiple versions of himself. I can't ask him about it, though. He doesn't know about his baby in his storyline, yet. And it's been a fucking hard secret to keep from him, hiding my laptop every time I write Shannon's chapters so he can't get a sneak peek when he visits me.

Stepping sideways, I lean out the bathroom door to glance at the black alarm clock on my oak bedroom dresser.

8:42 p.m.

The girls are due to arrive soon.

I toss the lip stain back in the drawer and run the straightening iron over my hair. I'd been planning on cutting at least six inches off my waist-length red-brown hair again. It's easier to deal with when it's shorter, but a certain someone who really enjoys burying his hands in it, grabbing and pulling it—yeah, you know I'm talking about Loki—convinced me to leave the length. Since I happen to enjoy what he does when he yanks my hair, I agreed. Still, it takes me longer than I'd like to straighten the heavy auburn mass. If I wasn't going out, I'd let the curls run amok.

Finally done and clad only in my thong, I head into my walk-in closet to take my royal blue dress from its hanger. With my hand on the dress, I pause. God, it's been a while since I've gone out. Not since the New Year's party with friends four months ago, although they were here for that barbeque a few weeks back. Now I know you remember that one... where Thor rocked my world, and then Loki showed up afterward to tie me to my hammock.

Even the memory has me shivering, my bare nipples tightening. Talk about seeing fucking galaxies.

The mid-thigh length dress hugs all my ample curves as I tug the stretchy fabric over my head. It shows a lot of skin, with an open middle consisting of a few criss-cross straps to hold the top and bottom together, and a straight, but low square neckline. With a mostly open back, I'm relying on the built-in bra to keep my generous chest in place and avoid a wardrobe malfunction.

Checking in the full-length mirror on the bedroom wall to ensure the straps aren't twisted in the back, I grin and wiggle my hips. It's the kind of dress that would make Loki growl and toss me on his shoulder to carry me to the bedroom. As sexy as it makes me feel, it's probably good Loki isn't coming tonight or I'd never make it to the club.

Guilt twists in my gut and I push a hand against it. Earlier this week, I told him I was going out with friends and wouldn't be available tonight, but I didn't tell him it would be his consort and two Asgardian Valkyrie joining me. I hate misleading him.

But damn it, he's been too gentlemanly since the hammock incident. I have no defences against the way my heart melts at his tender lovemaking. I'm getting too attached. There's no way Loki loves me, despite the feeling I get when he touches me. It's got to be my hormones running amok. He's not meant for me and even though he and Shannon don't feel their soulmate connection in this reality, I'll always know he isn't really mine. In their universe, she is his entire world. My hand clenches into a fist, pressing harder into my stomach as I stare at my reflection and meet my own green eyes with their golden brown centres flaring out from the dark pupil, windows to my vulnerability. I can't lose sight of that truth.

"He's not mine. I can't be his." I can't let myself forget that, no matter how often he claims me as his in this reality. My eyes turn glassy in the reflection and I blink, then blink again. No way am I ruining my make-up, or the fun I'm having now by being stupid. Damn it, I need him to return to fucking me senseless with savage intensity.

"Sex... just sex." And maybe if I tell myself that often enough, I'll be able to make my foolish heart believe it.

A feminine voice drifts up from my foyer. "Melody? Are you here?" Unlike certain rude males that pop into whatever room they want, or even watch me when I can't see them, the girls tend to use my main house entrance and announce themselves.

"I'll be right down!" I shout, fanning my hands in front of my face as I blink the last of the emotion away and plaster a smile on my face. After snagging my silver stiletto heels in my fingertips, I run lightly down the wooden stairs in my bare feet, then hug Shannon, Mist, and Kara when I get to the bottom.

"Do you need anything from here, or are we good to go?" I slip on my heels when they nod and check my phone. "The Uber will be here in just a couple of minutes."

"Sounds great. I assume that means you will be drinking and dancing with us?" Shannon asks, hazel eyes lighting in anticipation. She rotates her waist and pops a hip as she dances in place, her little black dress flaring from her waist and swirling around midthigh.

Her enthusiasm is infectious and I can't help but smile for real this time. "Oh absolutely! I've been looking forward to this for several weeks now." Or at least, since those days of tender aftercare rang alarm bells within me. A nervous shiver crawls through my chest. I need some emotional and physical distance from Loki. Desperately. Time to rebuild my armour.

"Good, because you look absolutely stunning, Melody." Kara wraps an arm around me, hugging me to her taller frame. "I'm expecting us to have a fantastic time."

"Definitely. It wasn't easy giving the guys a slip to get here, let me tell you!" complains Mist with a toss of sapphire locks and an eye roll. She wrinkles her nose and tugs me free of Kara to hug me herself.

Why would they notice? Shouldn't they be within their story timeline? Forcing a laugh, I push the uneasiness within me to the side and focus on the girls. "You'd think he'd be content with the chapters I've given the two of you lately." I wink at Shannon, carefully not saying Loki's name out loud. The last thing I need tonight is to draw his attention.

She shrugs a shoulder and smiles ruefully. "You know how he is. It just fires him up, instead of wearing him out."

It boggles my mind how she can recall the events but still have no real emotional reaction to them when she's here. How can she not crave Loki with every cell of her body? He's a sensual master and never, ever leaves anyone unsatisfied. "True. Let's just avoid any reference to his name, okay? I've had a quiet couple of weeks while I've kept him busy with you, after I managed to get myself in... well... let's say he was quite thorough in his lesson on how much he really doesn't like sharing." I fan myself, heat stirring in my abdomen just thinking about it.

Mist quirks an eyebrow at me. "I definitely want to hear this story."

"And... our ride is here!" I open the front door, ushering them out and into the car. It's a short twenty-minute drive from my home on the lake into the nearby city and the club, and I keep redirecting the conversation every time they try to convince me to tell them what Loki's lesson involved. Instead, I put Shannon on the spot, getting them to ask the ways in which Loki settled Odin's gift into her genetic structure. I already know, of course, but Mist and Kara don't, so that's half the fun.

There's a long line waiting to get into Club Illusion when we arrive, but as we start to walk towards the shining black door with silver trim, the heavily muscled bouncer waves us forward.

"C'mon, ladies. Beauties like you don't need to wait." He unclips the red velvet rope and lets us by. "Have a great time tonight."

Thanking him, we pass through the doors, drop our jackets at the coat check, and head to the gleaming black bar curving in a circle on the right side of the expansive space. Strobe lights flash, reflecting off silver mirror strips hanging from the ceiling and the dance floor lights with images across its surface, changing from rippling water to a dark forest, then an alien city before I look away. At this hour, the music is already thumping with a heavy beat that makes you want to move. I feel it in my chest, vibrating my body.

"Shots?" I ask, and Shannon immediately nods.

"Absolutely. Three Wise Men all around," Shannon orders from one of the black and white-clad bartenders, catching his eye as he spins bottles in the air.

Mist and Kara look at us, eyebrows raised.

"It's a whiskey shot. You'll like it," I tell them.

"What's a shot?" Kara asks.

"It's an alcoholic drink. It comes in a small glass, and you drink it back in one mouthful, instead of sipping it like you might another beverage," Shannon explains.

I pass the glasses around as the bartender sets them out with a flourish.

"Hold them like this, then we say something, usually '*cheers*', and we all drink it back at the same time. Ready?" I tell them, waiting for them to nod, and we toss the shot back. It's pure whiskey, three kinds together, and it burns its way down in a smooth heat.

"Woo! I liked that. *Another!*" Kara yells.

I laugh at her boisterous approval and signal the bartender for another round.

Mist peruses the shot menu listed in flowing lights on a screen above the bar. It's one of the reasons I like coming here. They have one hundred different kinds. We try a Washington Apple, then an Irish Slammer, and a Perverted Irishman before I call a temporary halt.

I'm not foolish enough to match drinks with Asgardians.

CHAPTER TWENTY-FOUR

Friends & Lovers

A wave of lightheadedness has me swaying and clutching at the bar. "Okay, I know you all can drink me under the table, but how about we dance for a bit so I can recover? I can't do more shots for a while if you want me conscious." The first ones are already hitting me. I definitely need to burn off some of this alcohol. "Although, you can certainly have more without me," I add when Kara blinks in surprise.

Shannon nods and slams down her shot glass. "Agreed! Let's dance!" She grabs my hand and starts leading me to the dance floor through the crowd of bodies. Kara and Mist follow close behind. Finding space, we rock, swivel our hips, sway, and bump to the blend of tunes put out by tonight's DJ. Despite them not having this kind of music on Asgard, Kara and Mist have obviously been out dancing on Earth in recent decades, and Shannon is certainly no slouch either. She shouts out some lyrics with the more popular songs. It's yet another example of things I didn't know about my own characters. They continue to surprise me, surpassing the limits of my original character sketches.

"Water break!" I call out over the music when it changes to a hip-hop song I'm not thrilled with. "Who wants water?"

"I'll help you grab some for all of us. Kara, why don't you and Mist see if you can grab us a high top or a booth?" Shannon says, gesturing towards the walls surrounding the dance floor opposite the busy bar area. "If we want someplace to sit, we need to stake our claim now before it gets even more packed in here."

She and I head over to the bar. It's chaotic with people at least three deep waiting along the length to order but it doesn't take long before the same bartender that served us before arrives, leaning forward and flirting with Shannon. She curls a long auburn strand around a finger and gazes at him through her lashes. "Four bottles of water, four Lemon Drops, and four Old Fashioneds," she orders, looking back at me with a wink.

When he moves away to make them, I can't help teasing her. "He's cute. Interested?"

She laughs, raising her hand, palm facing me. "Oh no. Not at all. Thanks to Loki scratching that itch quite thoroughly, I'm good. Not feeling the need, and I know you know exactly what I mean." She smirks and cocks her head, tapping her lips. "Although, if I did, that bartender would definitely be in the running. Did you see the tight ass on him?"

I snort and cover my mouth, shoulders shaking as I laugh.

Shannon's smile widens and she shrugs, completely unrepentant.

The bartender returns with our drinks, and between us, we manage to carry them.

"Do you see them?" I'm searching, rising to my tiptoes to try to see through the crowd, but haven't spotted Kara and Mist yet.

Shannon jerks her head to the left. "Unbelievably, it looks like they snagged a booth over in the corner. I wonder who they intimidated?"

It's a challenge making our way there as we weave around people, and I sigh, shoulders dropping as I slide the drinks I'm holding onto the black reflective table without spilling. A minor miracle in itself. "Hey, you two lovely ladies. So Shannon and I are wondering where you stashed the bodies to get a corner booth back here?"

They look at each other and smirk, giving nonchalant shrugs.

Shannon snorts. "Yeah, not sure we believe you. Melody and I are far more familiar with nightclub dynamics. You definitely had to scare someone off to get this table," she says as she slides into the large curved booth.

Mist laughs and nods towards a bouncer standing in the shadows at the wall near an emergency exit. "I just took advantage of his interest, and he got us our table." She brushes her blue hair back from her face in a seductive rake of her fingers.

"Good god, I can't believe I've unleashed you two on my unsuspecting world," I tease.

Mist flutters her lashes at me. She is spectacularly beautiful with her unusual tricoloured blue eyes that flow from the darkest ocean to a bright sunny sky, rimmed by indigo. I fully expect some woman to demand to know where Mist got her contacts. Pixie-like with her delicate features despite her height topping me by multiple inches, it is easy to see how others fail to notice the lethal strength, intelligence, and dancer's flexibility currently encased in a slinky silver dress that makes her such an effective defender of Asgard.

"So, what are these?" Kara asks, waving a graceful finger at the drinks and drawing my attention from my perusal of Mist.

Shannon pushes the bright yellow Lemon Drops and clear amber Old Fashioneds to each of us. "The shot is vodka and lemon, and the drink is whiskey and orange. You'll like both."

We toss the shot back and agree. It's good. Too good, frankly. I could see myself drinking way too many of these.

"So Mist, other than the bouncer, who's caught your eye lately?" Shannon asks, lips quirking.

I open my bottle of water, sipping to hide my grin.

Mist winks. "Oh, you know. I don't kiss and tell."

Kara almost snorts her drink out her nose. "What a *liar*! You do too! Come on. Who is it lately? One of the

Einherjar? A fellow Valkyrie? Or did you find someone when you were on Vanaheim a few weeks ago?"

Shannon and I look at each other, eyes widening with matching grins.

Mist rolls her eyes. "I don't *always* pick up someone."

Kara brushes back her red curls and arches an elegant eyebrow. "Right. Sure. Tell that to someone who hasn't known you for hundreds of years."

Mist laughs and gives Kara a sidelong glance through her lashes. "Okay, fine. Yes. I saw your sister, and when we went out for drinks, she introduced me to an acquaintance. He was fun. I might see him again next time I'm there. Or maybe I'll just get together with your sister," she teases.

Kara scowls, crumples up her drink napkin, and tosses it at Mist. "Leave my twin off your list of conquests, bitch."

Mist sticks her tongue out. "Make me. Maybe I want to compare sisters."

They both crack up laughing. I glance over to see Shannon, her head propped on her fist, watching them with fascination. She doesn't know them very well yet, but I hide my smile, aware of just how important Mist and Kara will become to her.

"So, you two were together at some point?" Shannon asks.

Kara shakes her head, sending her curls bouncing, still chuckling. "Yes, but we decided we are better as friends than lovers, not that it stops us from enjoying each other once in a while when the mood strikes. Mist is more of a browser than I am, though."

I snort at the term. It's hilarious. I'm definitely going to remember it and use it.

"*Me?* I'm sure it was *you* I saw riding stick in the palace stable hayloft when I got back from Vanaheim. One of the Einherjar, or did you seduce a stableman?" Mist taunts.

"I might prefer pussy, but every once in a while, I want a hard cock. He had a good, thick one and decent stamina." Kara smirks and raises an eyebrow. "Of course, nothing like fucking a fertility god, right Shannon? Melody? You two wouldn't have any experience you want to share with us about *that*, now would you?" She beacons with her fingers. "Come on, details please."

"You know, that is so very true! Melody has ridden *both* royal stallions. How exactly did *that* happen, since everyone knows that Loki doesn't like to share?" Mist asks, putting me in the blazing centre of the spotlight.

CHAPTER TWENTY-FIVE
In Over My Head

I choke on my spit. Yeah, I don't want to go there, but pinned in the light, I can't escape. Tipping up my water bottle, I gulp it down. I'm stalling for time as my insides churn and sweat breaks out on my neck.

"She swallows pretty well, don't you think? Why do I feel like our princes would agree?" Kara teases, leaning on her elbow to focus entirely on me.

Damn it, I'm doing my best to not remember, to not think of the memories their words evoke. But I can't escape them and my face flushes with heat, warmth crawling up my neck until my cheeks blaze and even my ears feel on fire.

I put the empty bottle down, dragging my gaze from theirs as I fidget.

"Damn, and I thought I blushed," Shannon says, amusement colouring her tone. "Besides, as our writer, you get to know the details of our sex lives when they are on the page. It's *only fair* you share a few with us, so we can also live vicariously through yours."

I groan and put my hand over my face, then peeking at them through my fingers. Nerves churn in my belly. They are not letting this go. All three eagerly await my answer, staring at me. "What exactly is it you want to know?" I ask hesitantly.

God, my stomach wants to sink to the floor. Just like Han Solo, I have a really bad feeling about this. Somehow, some way, I'm going to pay for this indiscretion.

"So, was it both at the same time?" Mist asks, tapping the table, then making rude hand gestures as she portrays the potential combinations.

I gulp. "They took turns." My voice squeaks on the last word as I squirm. Why is it so much easier to write than to say?

Kara smirks. "Who's bigger?"

I gnaw on my lip. Damn it. This is going to bite me in the ass somehow. I just know it. I can almost feel Loki's glare on my neck, that predatory swagger as he stalks me, but there's no one but the bouncer behind us. Still, I can barely get the whisper out. "Thor's thicker."

Mist punches Kara in the shoulder. "*Ha!* I win the bet. I told you! It's all in the forearms."

Kara rolls her eyes. "Yeah. Fine. You have more experience with cocks than I do, anyway."

"Who's better?" Mist asks, eyes gleaming.

I slap my hands over my face and groan. Fanfuckingtastic. How the hell do I answer that? No way can I answer that! I've never seen Thor angry, but I know his character sketch too well, and I'm not about to poke him in his pride. I'd really like the building to remain standing. Hell, I've already risked too much by saying his name even once. No way am I saying Loki's name. I don't want to draw *either* of their attention tonight. Finally, I blurt, "Neither has ever left me unsatisfied." There. Diplomatic.

Kara laughs and winks. "That's not what we asked, although it's good that neither are selfish bastards. You'd hope our royal princes would be good in the sack. Asgard's reputation on the line, diplomatic relations, and all that."

"Come on, Melody. Be honest." Mist leans forward on the table as she asks, "Which one is more inventive, thorough, and has you cumming the fastest?"

Through my fingers, my eyes meet Shannon's. She grins. She knows my answer. I can't stop the little smile that twitches my lips, despite my hot face.

"It's totally Loki, isn't it?" she says, holding my gaze.

I nod once, a quick movement of my head.

Mist and Kara hoot, banging their glasses on the table.

"The two of you sure are close-mouthed about what he actually does to drive you so wild. What are you so worried about? Will he punish you if you talk? Tie you up and spank you? Break out the whips, chains, and nipple clips?" Mist teases.

Shannon's eyes return to mine, both of us unable to say a word. She knows, even though he hasn't pushed her beyond some light bondage yet in what I've written for her. I know she knows. It's in his eyes, his dominance, his dirty talk that is enough to light a fire before he even touches a woman.

Kara's mouth drops open, eyes widening. "By the Norns! *You are*!"

Mist is barely able to talk between bursts of laughter. "I was just... guessing... he kinda has... dangerous vibe... but *damn girls*! Kinky!" Getting a hold of herself, she tries to keep a straight face. "Okay, I've gotta give our prince props. That's fucking hot. Well done, Loki!" She salutes him with her glass before taking a drink.

I wince. Fucking hell, they need to stop saying his name. Maybe he doesn't notice when they say it, but still. Before they ask more, I need to change the topic. I have no idea how Loki or Thor will feel about us discussing them like this, but I can only imagine Loki's punishment if he finds out. I toss back my Old Fashioned. "Okay, before you get me in more trouble than I can handle, how about we dance?"

Kara and Mist stand, but Shannon shakes her head, pushing their glasses towards them.

"No, you two need to finish your drinks first. It's not safe to leave drinks without someone at the table to watch them. It's probably not an issue with your Asgardian metabolism, but assholes could slip date rape drugs into your drink if you leave it and then come back to drink it," she tells them. "We don't want to chance it either way."

I nod when their eyes widen, then scowls darken their features.

"That's disgusting!" Mist says.

"Agreed." Kara wrinkles her nose. "We'd tear them apart for trying."

"While I'm sure you would, let's not start a diplomatic incident, okay?" I ask, imagining the chaos that would erupt if cops were to try to arrest one of my characters who then disappear right in front of him. How the hell would I answer that if they asked me to explain? Would I get arrested as an accomplice?

They swallow their drinks quickly, and we head back out onto the dance floor. Mist swings by the bouncer, and I see him nod to her, agreeing to save our table I assume when he walks over to stand in front of it, arms crossed. I'd been so desperate to escape their questions that I hadn't even considered we might lose the table. What did she promise him? Or did she just charm him into doing it for her?

We have dance moves galore, getting into the beat, playing off each other's choices, challenging and echoing them back. Guys try to cut in a few times, and we flick them off, some more harshly than others. Eventually, I notice Kara, Mist, and Shannon have surrounded me, keeping me in the middle. I don't mind their protectiveness. As immortals, they're a lot tougher than me. I might write fight sequences, but they actually know it. They have no trouble rebuffing even the most persistent of handsy drunk men, whereas I have more difficulty. If only I had their reflexes.

When the shooter girls come around with racks of colourful shots, we have a few more rounds out on the dance floor. Everything gets a bit blurry, light swirling around me in the artificial smoke they pump into the air and I call a halt to mine while the girls continue with more rounds. I can't keep up with them, and I know it.

Then, it is back to dancing again.

It seems to get even more crowded on the dance floor. People press in from all sides, and it's harder to find space to move. Kara pulls me in tight, as Mist dances against my back, pinning me between the two strong Valkyrie. Dizziness has me clinging to them and the floor's shifting images don't help at all. I lose track of Shannon, then spot her at the bar, talking to the flirty bartender.

I can't tell whose hands are whose anymore. One arm is wrapped around Kara's neck, and I think Mist is holding that hand, but maybe it's Kara. My other is around her waist, and someone's hands are on the bare skin of my waist and abdomen.

Wait... whose hands are cupping my breasts? Distracted by that thought, suddenly Kara is kissing me.

It isn't the first time I've kissed a girl, but I'll admit my experience is limited. Her lips are soft, featherlight as she touches her lips to mine, once, twice, and a third time. The curves pressing and sliding against my front and back are soft, supple but strong, and so different from my own plush form. I'm not in shape like the Valkyrie with their constant fight training.

Kara draws back, meeting my eyes.

Smiling at her blurry face, I let go of the hand I'm holding at her nape to wrap my fingers in her curly red locks cascading down her back. Everything is kind of spinning.

Her gaze focuses behind me. An amused smirk stretches her lips. "I wondered how long it would take," she says, eyes twinkling.

CHAPTER TWENTY-SIX
Double Trouble

"This should be interesting," Mist whispers into my ear as she releases me and steps away from my back, only to be replaced by a taller female form.

"Shannon?" I ask, confused as a pair of hands caress over my bare sides, sliding under the straps at my abdomen. I don't remember Shannon being so much taller than I in our heels. My head is a bit fuzzy, though, so maybe I'm wrong.

"No, Shannon is flirting with the bartender and ordering another round of drinks and shots for your table and *friends*," a female voice purrs in my ear.

I stiffen, pulse pounding frantically at something in the woman's tone as Kara steps back to allow a tall, willowy woman with gorgeous, straight, long, ebony hair to take her place. She turns to face me, and I'm caught by her model-perfect features with high cheekbones, red lips, dark brows, and gorgeous green eyes that contrast with her pale skin. She is breathtakingly beautiful.

I'm stunned. Mouth open. So much so that I'm allowing the woman behind me to sway my body with the music. Okay, some of that might also be all the alcohol I've consumed. I blink up at the supermodel in front of me, and she smiles. My eyes widen, and a squeak escapes my lips. I recognize that smirk and the look in those half-lidded emerald eyes.

"Who?" I turn in the arms holding me to see the exact same expression and features on the woman behind me.

Oh. My. God.

It's not twins. Nope. My life would obviously never be so plebeian. Twins would be easy to handle in comparison. All the alcohol in the world isn't going to help me now. I'm completely and utterly fucked. And probably literally too if she has her way... god, she always has her way.

"Safe word?" she asks, holding my wide-eyed gaze.

"Red," I respond, automatically.

"Right now?"

"Green," I reply, my voice turning breathless.

"You are sure? You haven't had too much alcohol to consent?" she asks, peering into my eyes.

She's not wrong. My thoughts had been on the fuzzy side until she showed up. Yet now, adrenaline has my heart racing and every sense sharpening. "Green," I confirm.

The woman behind me tucks me tighter against her body with a firm hand low on my bare abdomen, long fingers slipping under the edge of my dress, allowing her other hand to clasp the front of my neck. The woman in front presses her body into me, one hand fisting the hair at my nape, while the other traces up my arm in a delicate caress. She leans down to nip my lower lip before sliding her tongue along it in a recognizable stroke.

My whole body shudders in reaction, heating and melting into her touch. The whole situation is so unexpected that my body responds to the intimate touches and familiar possessive handling while my mind is still racing at the change.

She teases my lip again before kissing me deeper, drawing a moan out of me.

Another pair of lips kiss my neck, teeth nipping as she works her way up to my ear even as her hand squeezes my throat gently. "Figured it out yet?" she purrs in my ear before nipping my earlobe in a sharp flash of pain.

There's only one individual who holds me like this, handles my body exactly like this. But oh god, it's never been quite like this before. "Loki," I whisper as our lips break apart.

The Loki in front of me smiles, hand tugging my hair to give the Loki behind me better access to lick her way down my neck. "Clever little writer. You did insist on it being ladies' night tonight when you started dishing secrets to Kara and Mist."

"I didn't—" I protest, only to be stilled by the proprietary squeeze at my throat and punishing pinch to my nipples through the fabric of my dress. A whimper escapes me as the flash of pain travels to my sex, coiling heat in my abdomen.

"Are you seriously trying to lie to the Goddess of Chaos, darling?" A hand moves up my inner thigh, fingertips sliding under the thong and into the wet heat between my legs.

I moan. Holy fuck, it's hard to think with fingers tugging at taut peaks, mouths licking and biting my neck, while other fingers pump teasingly in and out over sensitive nerves.

"I asked you a question, little writer," her voice growls. Male or female, Loki's dominance is unquestionable. She expects to be obeyed. Her fingers move faster, a thumb sliding over my clit in sensuous demand.

"Loki!" I whimper.

"Answer me now."

"Didn't lie."

"What did you say to them?"

Unable to stop writhing, I'm on the cusp of climaxing in her arms on the dance floor. Who the fuck cares who is around me? Not me, that's for damn sure. But the tone of her voice holds me back.

"Just—just that Thor is thicker... but—but that... *oh god*... you are better!" I finally manage between gasps. "Please, Loki. Please let me cum?" I ask, not wanting to get in more trouble.

"Yes, that *is* what you said, isn't it. Now, who does this sexy little body belong to? Is it those Valkyrie who took without asking?" she growls.

I try to shake my head, caught in her sensual claws, like a cat with a favourite toy. My mind swirls as I cling to her, desperately riding her fingers. Everything within me is tightening, coiling, and it's all I can do to hold on, hold it back.

"Answer me so I can give you what your little cunt is begging for. Let me hear your voice, little writer."

"You. I belong to you," I blurt out. My thighs quiver with electric flashes of sensation and heat flaring out from my abdomen in escaping bursts.

"Good girl. That deserves a reward, I believe." She purrs as the Loki behind me bites my neck hard. "Cum, darling."

My mouth opens as the cresting wave hits. She captures my lips and my shriek of pleasure, holding me upright as my knees give out and my body shakes. A leaf in a fall windstorm, I'm tumbled about in the erotic currents. Loki strokes me until my core stops pulsing and I catch my breath.

"My good little writer," she murmurs, then removes her fingers and snaps my thong off at the same time. Together, both Lokis lead my trembling form off the dance floor. Truthfully, they're almost carrying me as I can't seem to walk in my heels. If it wasn't for their grip on me, I'd crash into everyone on our path to the booth where Shannon, Mist, and Kara are talking, drinking, and watching us approach.

"Did you enjoy dancing with Loki, Melody?" Kara asks with an eyebrow raised and smirk on her lips.

Still panting, I don't get a chance to answer.

The Loki that is sliding into the booth first cuts me off with a glance. "She did," Loki says, putting my torn black thong on the table as she turns to face the others.

CHAPTER TWENTY-SEVEN

What's On The Menu?

Even if they can't see it in the dark club, my cheeks are hot. I could claim it was from dancing, but they would never let me get away with that lie. Shannon has her hand over her mouth, trying not to laugh as her eyes dance. Kara bites her lip to not laugh but I can see her eyes watering from across the damn table. Mist grins widely. The first Loki tugs me along the curved bench seat so the second Loki can sit beside me, sandwiching me between them.

"So how much trouble is Melody in, Loki?" Mist asks, reaching for my thong. "Will you be tying her up? Breaking out the whips?"

"Oh no. Not this time," Loki taunts, snatching the scrap of fabric out of Mist's reach. A flash of black seidhr and my thong disappears from Loki's palm. I guess I'm not getting it back and her tone has me shifting in my seat.

Slickness coats my sex and I'm trying to not notice the second heartbeat pulsing within my core.

Loki's hand slides up my upper thigh under the table.

Oh god. Clearly, she has more planned for me than the display on the dance floor.

Pulse fluttering in my throat, I glance at her, and she flashes me a wickedly erotic little smile as her eyes flicker to me for a second. Needing something to do with my hands as my stomach twists with nerves, I take a drink of the water bottle Shannon passes to me. She's trying to change the topic. She recognizes the look in Loki's eyes. That smile means trouble.

I choke when Loki's fingers tug at my thigh to open my legs.

Instead, I press my thighs together.

One hand from each Loki tugs my legs apart. She's not going to be denied as her fingers trace over my passion-drenched skin, delving into me. Yet, I'm not going to say 'red' either, even though I know she'll stop in an instant if I use my safe word. I know the rules after I've consented.

And after a few weeks of gentlemanly sex with Loki, I want her to do her worst. This is want I asked for, wasn't it? The dirtier, the better, even if I have no idea how far she will push me. I love when Loki gets like this. It's a craving in my blood and I need my fix.

I lock my muscles just as she tweaks the hard knot of nerves at my center. With my face flushing, I fight to control my breathing, to not let my hips jerk in reaction.

Part of me wants to scream at the building flames searing my sex.

Kara gives me a funny look, eyes scanning my heated face. "How's your martini?"

I blink a couple of times as two of Loki's fingers start thrusting. Fuck. There is no way I'll be able to hold out long.

With a shaking hand, I reach for and take a sip of the drink. "It's great... I'm just a bit warm from the dancing," I manage in a calm but breathless voice.

A fine shudder escapes my control before I can put the glass down, and I slosh the drink, spilling a bit over the side and onto the table.

"Warm, huh?" Kara looks at the Loki on my right, whose face is completely bland, tilting her head at Kara's perusal. Yet the heat in her emerald eyes gives her away as she thoroughly fucks me with her fingers in front of everyone.

Unable to hold still, I grab the table to prevent a moan from escaping.

Kara arches an eyebrow at Loki. "Are you fingering our writer at the table, Loki?"

A slow smile on both Lokis' faces answers her question.

Mist's eyes widen and she grins. "Is this her punishment?"

"Yes. She knows she's not allowed to cum until I allow it," the Loki on my left replies. "And you will beg, won't you, even with them here?" she asks me.

I'm trembling, clinging to the table with a death grip as the flames burn wider, and it takes me a few tries to answer without a whimper escaping. "Yes, Loki."

The Loki on my right with her fingers buried in me adds, "But it's not just her punishment. It's yours as well."

"Ours?" asks Mist.

Kara frowns. Shannon just covers her smile, looking away.

"Yes, yours. You see how gorgeous Melody is in her arousal." She shifts the angle of her fingers, and a soft squelching sound accompanies every thrust. Another wave of heat flashes over my skin, gooseflesh rising but I'm too aroused to care, too busy panting and trying to keep the orgasm at bay. Shudders wrack my torso.

Kara's eyes widen.

Loki smirks. "Yes, that's how wet she is. Her little cunt is flushed, soaked, and so very soft to the touch. It feels absolutely incredible wrapped hot and tight around my fingers."

I keen, unable to stay silent as her thumb rubs over my clit with each stroke.

Mist looks into my eyes. Even as distracted as I am with my impending climax, I recognize the flush of arousal on her cheeks and dilated pupils.

"Please Loki," I beg quietly, my fingers whitening in their grip on the table.

"You want to cum, don't you," she taunts.

"Yes, Loki. Please. Please let me cum," I whimper.

"Would you let me spread you out on this table and eat you, sucking up all those delicious juices?" Loki asks.

I moan, trying to think. "Will the whole club be able to see me or just this table?" Loki likes to push my boundaries, but she also isn't a fan of sharing, so I'm pretty sure I know the correct answer.

The Loki on my left chuckles. "Smart girl. You know I'd never let the people out there see this pretty pussy. It's mine. But I will punish our Valkyrie by enjoying you in front of them. They tried prying for information and got intimate on the dance floor after plying you with drinks. They didn't ask you first when you were sober. You haven't given yourself to them and aren't in a relationship with them. You don't have their tolerance for alcohol and they should know better. Consent is required. *Never* let anyone take without asking, little writer."

"Yes, Loki," I agree, barely able to get the words out over the fire in my blood.

She turns my head to capture my lips in a kiss that is all tongue and erotic passion.

Our lips part as I gasp for breath.

"Cum for me, little one, and then I will feast on you," the Loki on my right commands as her fingers plunge harder and faster.

"Loki!" I shriek as the climax rips through me, exploding me to the far reaches of the cosmos, like the birth of a star flaring heat outward.

When my senses return, Loki continues to stroke me until my limbs stop shaking. Then with a careless wave towards the club, a shimmering transparent wall appears.

"We can see out, but no one can see in," Loki confirms when I meet her gaze, answering my unspoken question.

The Loki on my left rises and pulls me from the seat, laying me on the table. The other Loki stays in her seat but takes my hands, holding them pinned above my head.

She slowly raises the hem of my dress up to my abdomen. "Put your feet on my shoulders and spread your knees for me, darling."

My stomach quivers with nerves and a heady dose of rekindled excitement that chases away the satiation in my body. I slowly lift my feet, one at a time, laying them on Loki's shoulders. Taking my time, I spread my knees.

Kara sucks in a breath. "Damn. Glistening like dew. Gorgeous."

Loki bends her head down and breathes in. "Such a fine bouquet. A hint of sweet apple wood smoke." She places butterfly-soft kisses along my inner thighs, even as her thumbs lightly stroke over tender skin.

I squirm, unable to keep my hips still. God, I love when Loki decides to eat me.

"You are such a tease, Loki," complains Mist. She leans up on the table, braced on her hands and watching every move the Loki between my thighs makes.

"Melody has learned that sometimes delaying what you want makes it so much more pleasurable in the end. Haven't you, little one?" Loki asks, meeting my eyes.

The memory of how Loki edged me for hours, not letting me orgasm while he'd played with me and kept me on the precipice has my spine arching. I've never climaxed so hard or so many times in a row as I did the day Loki taught me the benefits of delayed gratification. "Yes." My voice is a breathless whisper of sound.

Her eyes narrow slightly. "Yes, what?"

"Yes, Loki," I reply obediently, forcing my voice louder despite my panting.

She gives me a half smile as her thumbs trace around my opening. Then, lowering her head, she flicks over my clit with a stiff tongue, and my hips jerk off the table at the electric sensation. Long lapping strokes of her tongue along both sides tantalize as one thumb dips just inside in tiny shallow thrusts. Unable to stay still, my toes point.

"Mmm... so delicious. Can you smell her arousal, Valkyrie?" Loki asks between tasting licks that have me squirming, trying to bring my sex up to her taunting mouth.

"Yes," Kara whispers and Mist nods.

"I don't think I heard you, Valkyrie. What was that?" Loki demands, her voice a sensual growl.

"Yes, Princess," Kara and Mist answer together, their voices strained.

Turning my head, even my passion-glazed eyes can see their cheeks are flushed, eyes focused on what Loki is doing to me as their hands move on each other. Glancing from them to Shannon, she's also red-cheeked and her eyes are wide, watching. A stray thought flits through my mind. Has she ever been with a woman before?

The Loki holding my hands raises an eyebrow. She follows my gaze, smiles slightly, then glides her hands down my arms in a sensuous caress, and lowers her head to my ear. "Would you give Shannon a taste if she wants one?" she purrs in a murmur.

"Yes," I gasp as the other Loki plunges two fingers into me and sucks my clit into her mouth. Electricity spikes within me and my back twists off the table, a loud keening cry escaping. Long fingers pull down the top of my dress, freeing my breasts for Loki's fingers to caress, twist, and pinch. I whimper at the sparking flares. She knows exactly how to play my body, and she does love to play.

But I want to play, too. I want to explore this aspect of Loki I haven't yet experienced.

"Please... please Loki, let me touch you?" I beg, my hands straining against her hold to reach for her.

"What is it you want?" the Loki above me asks, nibbling at my ear, as the Loki between my thighs nips my clit lightly and continues her slow penetration.

Despite the buzzing in my nerves as she raises my arousal, I grit my teeth to get the words out. "Let me do the same to you. Ride... my mouth... my fingers," I manage to say between gasps. Either Kara or Mist groans, but I'm too focused on Loki to figure out which one. It's so rare for Loki to let me have any control.

Raising her head, she smiles down at me and without stopping or slowing down what they're doing, the two Lokis shift my body further along the table so my head is hanging off where Loki sits. After rising onto her knees, she lifts her black dress and straddles my face.

I push her legs wider with my hands and lightly run a finger over her dampness, tugging her thong out of the way. She's radiating heat. It makes her familiar woodsy citrus scent stronger and there are more citrus notes in her current gender. I breathe deep, pulling it into my lungs with a hum of pleasure. Dipping two fingertips into the opening of her sheath, she's already slippery. Stealing the move she's used on me, I flick my tongue at her clit at the same time as I drive both fingers in, curling into her tight heat.

She clenches around my fingers as I flick harder with my tongue, and her moan resonates against my own core from the Loki between my thighs. Do both of her bodies feel it? How does she manage both at once? She could take the idea of masturbation to a whole new level.

Starting a rhythm I'm aching for her to copy after all her teasing, I plunge in and out. A flash of glee spears me when she mimics my movements and our moans rise and fall together. I flatten my tongue to lathe longer strokes over her. She's salty and sweet at the same time. And so very soft. The lack of steely rigidity under my tongue yet the same taste and scent is both familiar and confusing.

I'm distracted from my exploration of her by additional fingers driving in and out of me, paired with tentative licks. Loki is never tentative, but I can't glance down to see.

Loki's fingers start driving harder and faster, demanding my response and I copy her movements, the quivering in my thighs beginning that signals my impending orgasm.

Damn it, no! I want Loki to cum with me. With renewed desperation, I flick my tongue hard and fast.

When her sex starts to tremble, the roar of success has my spine arching. The boiling cauldron within me surges. We're both so close. It's right there. I strain not to let go, not orgasm first as I drive her harder. She hasn't given me permission yet. Every muscle within tightens, tension singing.

I've got to hold it back.

Not yet.

Oh god. Not yet.

She spasms around my fingers, and her hips jerk against my mouth. Moaning, she's grinding down on my fingers and face as she climaxes.

I'm whimpering, shaking with need as I lock my quivering muscles.

The scream presses on my throat as I fight to hold it back.

"Cum for me, little one."

I detonate, shrieking into her pussy as I writhe on the table. She lifts herself off my face, and I gasp, panting hard.

Still, she twists my nipples and drives her fingers into me, wrenching another orgasm out of me that has me scrambling for something to hold on to as my body bucks violently.

Finally, she slows, and I open my eyes to see Shannon lift her head from between my thighs with a smile. Loki pulls out their joined fingers and guides them to Shannon's mouth. She licks each one, sucking them into her mouth. Dipping her head back down, she darts her tongue into my still-trembling pussy a few times, making my body jerk with additional waves of sensation. When I stop shuddering, Shannon places a kiss on my core.

After standing up, she leans over me to kiss me lightly on the lips. "I agree with Loki. You taste amazing, Melody, and are absolutely gorgeous when you climax."

Loki smirks and pulls me up to sit, helping me fix my dress back in place after cleaning me with a wave of her hand.

CHAPTER TWENTY-EIGHT

Consequences

Kara sways in her seat. "Okay, lesson learned, Loki. Damn. I totally understand why you are a sex god," she pants, red-faced with her eyes slightly unfocused.

"Agreed!" chimes in Mist, looking dishevelled and shoving her hair from her sweaty face.

"Fertility goddess, but sure, sex god will due," Loki says with a negligent wave of her fingers.

"I have even more respect for you two, managing to keep up with Loki," Mists adds, looking at Shannon, then me.

Shannon grins while I chuckle and try to climb off the table, but my knees buckle like a newborn colt. Everything spins and distorts. Is it the club or me?

Loki catches me in her arms. "I think ladies' night is done for you, little writer. Would you like me to get you home?"

I nod, then glance around. There's only one Loki now. "What happened to the other you?"

She arches a dark eyebrow, her lips twitching. "Do I need two of myself to get you home? Are you planning on being a handful?"

I can't help but laugh. My head is still unsteady, the world tilting in front of me both from the alcohol and orgasms. I'm lucky I can even speak right now. Further mischief is absolutely *not* on the menu. "No. I have no nefarious or bratty plans currently."

She gives me a look, barely acknowledging the others as we say our goodbyes.

Yeah, Loki noticed I said *currently*, but hey, I'd be lying if I claim I'll never have plans like that. Of course I will. After all, how else will I get Loki to lose control?

Because you know I will.

What's life without a little danger and chaos, right? And when I'm too busy enjoying Loki's response, I'm not thinking about anything else, like things that can never be.

Securing me in her arms while still holding my gaze, she teleports us to my bedroom in several jumps. But with each one, my head gets dizzier. The little kernel of nausea worsens until it is a seething mass of wrongness within me. Pressing my hand to my belly, I swallow, then swallow again.

"You're looking a bit green. Are you going to vomit?"

I nod my head, not trusting myself to open my mouth. Saliva pools and the queasiness increases.

Quickly carrying me into the bathroom, Loki helps me to the toilet just as I begin to heave. It hurts, wrenching my body and burning my throat. She holds my long, tangled hair out of the way, rubbing my back through the first wave, then the second, and again through the third. Finally empty, my stomach still tries to turn itself inside out.

Shaking from the effort, it leaves a fine sweat coating my skin. To make me feel extra special, my head is absolutely splitting, like a spike pounding in my temples and behind my eyes.

With a flick of her hand, Loki conjures a glass of water and holds it to my mouth, helping me drink. I swish some in my mouth before spitting it out into the toilet, but she urges me to swallow some. God, it's a mistake. As soon as the water hits my stomach, it comes right back up, leaving me groaning.

"It would be cruel to point out you shouldn't attempt to match Asgardians in their ability to drink. I think you've figured that out for yourself. I hate seeing you like this, little one," Loki croons, rubbing my back as I lean against her while still maintaining a white-knuckled grip on the toilet.

My voice is a raspy whisper, with my throat burning. Fuck, it hurts to swallow. "I know. I didn't intend to. Guess I wasn't paying enough attention to what my body was telling me."

"Promise you won't do this to yourself again, and I'll take away the headache and nausea. I can't rid your system of all the alcohol. My healing abilities aren't that extensive, but I can help you that much." She holds my chin in her hands, meeting my eyes. "But only if you promise and keep your word. I won't enable you to hurt yourself like this."

A melting sensation in my chest has me smiling tiredly up at her blurry face. Hot tears trickle down my cheeks. "I promise I won't try to match Asgardians in their drinking. And I promise it's extremely rare for me to overdo my alcohol consumption to this extent. It's only ever gotten to this point once before in my life." When my grandma died and my rat-bastard of an ex cheated on me, not that I'll tell Loki that sad tale. I'm pathetic enough for one evening. "Not something I want to repeat. But I can't promise to never make a mistake. I'm not perfect, Loki."

She holds my gaze for a few moments, then her green eyes lighten with humour and the corner of her mouth twitches up. "Well now, that's about the most honest promise you could give me, isn't it?"

Loki leans closer, pressing her lips to mine. Warmth, with a hint of sex, surges through my body, creating a tingling sensation in its wake. My headache disappears, my tummy stops churning, and the nasty taste in my mouth dissipates, leaving her taste on my tongue. Even my dizziness is gone, and the room no longer spins. Our lips part, and she gently caresses my cheek, removing the last of my tears.

"All better?"

Damn. She's like the hangover cure fairy. If she could bottle that shit, she'd be a billionaire. "Yes. Thank you, Loki."

"Let's get you tucked into bed. I'm in the mood to snuggle this little mortal body of yours," she says as she pulls me to my feet.

With my head clear, I can walk myself now, but she doesn't release her grip on my hand. Instead, she tugs gently, guiding me to the bed.

"I take it you'd prefer to keep this sexy little dress?" she asks, eyes travelling over my body.

My lips quirk. "Yes. I like it."

"As do I. I particularly like the access it gives me, although I'm not sure how much I like others eying you in it," Loki growls, frowning down at the dress, then tugging a strap over my abdomen with a long finger.

As much as her response amuses me, I can't afford to enjoy it, to allow myself to fall into that trap. Exhaustion drags at my limbs, my body heavy and I rub my head, scowling at the reminder of truths I wish I didn't have to remember. "Loki, you don't own me." I pull my fingers from hers and cross my arms. We aren't even exclusive, I want to bite out, barely keeping the words from my lips.

"I may not own you outside of your bedroom, but in here, you are *mine*. Do you deny it?" Her green eyes narrow. "Do I need to prove just how much your little body belongs to me?"

"No," I grumble, letting out a heavy sigh. This isn't a battle I can win tonight, not that I really want to. I don't want to fight with her over things that can't be changed.

"Put your arms up for me."

Her eyebrow twitches when I hesitate and glare, then slowly raise my arms. In a move too fast for my tired eyes to follow, she's got the dress up and off me, leaving me naked. Snagging my nightshirt off the bed, she tugs it down over me.

"Into bed, little one. Come on, don't be cranky with me. I'm sorry I offended your sense of independence," Loki coaxes, even as she doesn't sound particularly sorry.

It's not that I necessarily mind Loki's possessiveness. After all, I absolutely enjoy that she feels that way about me. But it's one-sided. I can't ever claim Loki's sole affection. And I can't ever forget that, no matter how tempted I am to give in to the way I feel. I have to keep my head. It would hurt too much otherwise.

I crawl into bed, and she curls herself around me. Different from her male form with her breasts pressed into my back and softer curves, yet she still tucks my head into her shoulder, her leg between my thighs, and cups my breast in her palm. It's comforting, even though I know she'll be gone before I wake.

Loki never really stays and will never be mine.

Ready to continue this journey? Check out the sneak peek of Episode 5 – Fury Of The Storm.

About the Author

Melody Grace Hicks writes spicy science fantasy romance. She'd apologize for the increase in your lingerie replacement budget, but really, we both know it's those darn wickedly sexy males that bring you back for more, right? Born and raised on Canada's West Coast, Melody has travelled the world and brings this diversity into her fiction. By day, she's an award-winning internationally published scientist and professor, but at night, she dons her pen name to enthusiastically mash mythology and tell tales of soulmates, secret identities, unknown origins, betrayals, magical powers, polyamory, and love triangles.

If you enjoyed this story, there is much more to come (pun absolutely intended). In addition to the four episodes within this compilation, another eight episodes comprise the total of season one of Breaking The 4th Wall. You can get them individually, or in four-episode bundles with the second compilation, Ephemeral Pages (episodes 5-8), and the third complication, Fiction's Embrace (episodes 9-12). Check out the sneak peek of Episode 5—Fury Of The Storm in the following pages. These are a prelude to the full-length Triquetra Prophecy novels coming in later 2024, the first of the Gods Among Us Universe alluded to within these Breaking The 4th Wall tales. To stay up-to-date with the latest story releases and get a special bonus story, please subscribe to her email list on her webpage (melodygracehicks.com).

Melody loves interacting with her readers and you can follow her on Twitter (melodyghicks), Instagram and Facebook (melodygracehicks). Or, if you want to check out the first draft of her stories as she writes them and all kinds of bonus content, including uncensored one-shots and excerpts, join her on Ream (reamstories.com/melodygracehicks).

<u>A final note:</u> if you enjoyed this tale and want to see more from Melody, please do consider writing a review on Goodreads. It makes a huge difference in the ability of readers to find her stories.

Thank you for reading!

Also By Melody Grace Hicks

<u>**BREAKING THE 4TH WALL SEASON ONE**</u>
A Writer's Commitment – Episode 1
Delayed Gratification – Episode 2
Don't Taunt The Trickster – Episode 3
Ladies' Night – Episode 4
Seductive Characters - BT4W Season One (Episodes 1-4)
(paperback and ebook)
Fury Of The Storm – Episode 5
Birthday Party – Episode 6
After Party – Episode 7
Sub Drop – Episode 8
Ephemeral Pages – BT4W Season One (Episodes 5-8)
(paperback and ebook)
Road Trip – Episode 9
Giant Complication – Episode 10
<u>**OTHERS**</u>
30 Days To Save The World – Short Story Anthology

Sneak Peek

FURY OF THE STORM
Episode 5—Breaking the 4th Wall

When my fictional character saves me from a tornado, this erotic romance writer learns that harnessing nature might be more than she bargained for.

***

Who needs to chase storms when they find me all on their own? There is nothing more invigorating than watching a thunderstorm approach my home from across the lake. It's a spectacular display of weather that always gets my heart pounding. But really, I should know better than to rely on modern technology. After all, Grandma taught me the warning signs of dangerous storms. When Thor answers my call, the lessons he teaches give new meaning to harnessing the power of thunder and lightning. If I survive, it will be a hell of a ride.

Chapter One – Green Skies

My fingers fly over the keyboard, writing dialogue in the next scene of *Hidden,* when the power flickers in my office. It's enough to reset my internet signal. Annoying, but not the end of the world. Thank god I'm working on my laptop. There is nothing worse than writing a scene only to lose it to a power hiccup. With a glare at my router, I finish typing the sentences that are in my head and then peer out my window at the bright blue late afternoon sky.

Hmm... weird. Maybe someone hit a power pole, or they're doing work on the lines?

Diving back into the scene, I finish the conversation between my characters and move them on to their next scene. My neck is prickling though, hairs rising on my nape. It's distracting, splitting my focus. Something nags at my subconscious.

Setting my laptop aside, I get up to check my house for visitors. I don't smell any telltale citrus and wood, so it's not Loki lurking unseen. Probably. Trickster god? I snort. Maybe he should be the god of stalkers for as often as he shows up and stays invisible. He seems to enjoy spying on me.

I take another walk through my family room, kitchen, and foyer. Still no one. Actually, I haven't seen Loki since she tucked me in last week after that disastrous Ladies' Night, and disappeared before I woke. She doesn't usually stay away this long.

It's too bad.

I'd like to explore Loki's differences in her female form. Does she change her perspective on things, or have different priorities when in her other gender? But it's something that will have to wait. Loki's probably busy. My last chapter update to my beta-readers was only two days ago, and Loki discovered he's going to be a dad. I imagine he's pretty happy right now.

Still, something isn't quite right. The gooseflesh on my arms has yet to subside.

After walking through my kitchen and out the patio door to the backyard, I stop on the grass. The lake is calm, like glass, and there is no breeze. It's hot today, especially for late spring. The weather has been bouncing between warm and cold like a yo-yo. The air is sticky with humidity, and my off-the-shoulder white peasant blouse clings to my skin. I pull at the material, trying to get some air movement under my shirt. At least it's loose.

Maybe that's what's bothering me. It's too calm. It's rare for there to be no breeze at all.

A faint noise reaches me from across the water. The sky looks darker over there, like a smudge on the horizon beyond the far shore. Squinting into the distance, my suspicions are confirmed by a flash of light. It's a thunderstorm, headed towards me.

A surge of excitement crackles over my skin, and I wiggle my toes in the grass. I love thunderstorms with their warm rains, flashing lightning, and cracking booms of thunder. The power and wonder of them never fails to thrill me. We didn't have much in the way of thunderstorms when I was a little kid, before my parents died and grandma took me in. There just wasn't the clash of warm and cold fronts necessary to produce them. Instead, it rained. A lot. To the point that we'd joke it was liquid sunshine and good for the complexion.

But here, we get some incredible thunderstorms.

Padding across the soft grass in my bare feet to one of my wicker loveseats under my small pavilion shelter, I pull out the cushions from the storage box and get comfortable. Before she died, this was grandma's favourite place... well, only since she couldn't watch storms from her hot tub. She'd passed on her love of storms to me and the pavilion is the perfect spot to have a spectacular view of the storm.

It's both beautiful and eerie to watch the thunderstorm approach over the water. My yard is quiet and still. Everything is hushed, like all the birds, crickets, and frogs are holding their breath in anticipation. Yet the dark smudge has turned into a writhing, seething cauldron of ominous grey clouds forming a massive wall stretching far up into the sky.

Ripples disturb the reflection-like smoothness of the once-placid lake. The storm has reached the water on the far side, whipping up waves that are just starting to impact this shore. The white caps aren't visible, but there's a line of darker water moving closer.

Despite the humidity, the small hairs on my body stand, prickling over my skin. It's almost ticklish, and I rub my hands over my arms and legs to disrupt the sensation. The rumbles of thunder are audible now, echoing across the water as lightning flashes.

It's getting darker.

The sunlight falls to shadow as the sun disappears from sight behind the storm, hidden by the massive wall racing towards me from the west.

Way up in the sky above me, white clouds stretch like skeletal fingers towards this shore, pulled forward of the dark billowing and churning tower of rain-soaked turbulence. Around me, everything takes on a greenish cast, and I jolt upright from my relaxed lounge, pulse pounding with more than excitement as a tendril of alarm stiffens my spine and curls around my chest.

Green skies are never a good sign.

Acknowledgments

This book would never have seen the light of day without the support of numerous beta-readers, my fellow writers at WCX (writersconnx.com) and my wonderfully supportive daughter who listens to my ideas, critiques my graphics, and reads over my shoulder even when she shouldn't.